The Hunt

The Women of T.H.E.T.A. Book 3: Rebecca

By Elizabeth Borae

Dedication

Hey, Dad!
It's the 'See' game on a whole other level.
Thanks!

Author's Note

The Hunt contains spoilers for the previous book in the series, *Who Is Madalene?*. The journey is as entertaining as the resolution, but readers might prefer enjoying book two before diving into book three.

Happy Reading!

As the title suggests, this story has hunting elements. In keeping with the historical setting and personalities of the characters, hunting is done for food procurement. Anyone sensitive to such subjects, please proceed with caution.

Chapters

CHAPTER 1

The New Neighbor

Rebecca

Miss Rebecca Tarleton regained control of her breathing as she rubbed her throbbing hand. She'd been pawed at, harassed, and now this.

I'm not ready for the woods. I don't have my tools.

Rebecca had discovered too late that Lord Spencer wasn't the gentleman he'd seemed to be in London several months ago. She was a petite woman of twenty, but when he'd gotten too handsy, she'd given him a good punch and demanded he leave her be.

And he did.

But now, she was by herself in the forest, the place of her nightmares. Rebecca thought she'd conquered this, but then she hadn't been here without her equipment since those horrible few days when she was young.

Objectively, the woods were safe, serene, and beautiful, especially on this pleasant autumn day. Alone in the blackness of night was a different story. The terror had been etched on her for years.

The fear was tenfold, and Rebecca whimpered as the memories crept upon her, even though it was broad daylight. She usually prepared herself mentally and physically when she came to the woods, but Lord Spencer had driven them out here unexpectedly.

Breathe and think. Rebecca had survived the forest and became the stronger for it. She'd taught Lord Spencer a lesson, and hopefully, he'd think twice before treating another lady in like manner.

The clopping of horse hooves drifted through the air, and Rebecca craned her neck towards the sound. *Perhaps I can get a ride back since I'm not in the best state to do so on my own.*

Mr. Kenneth Barclay rounded the bend on his horse.

Rebecca's heart slammed. *I'm not the damsel in distress type, but I've never been so glad to see him.* "What are you doing here?" she called out.

"I'm headed to Laidley Park." Barclay slowed his horse to a stop near her. "Is no one with you?"

"I wasn't keen on the direction in which my outing with Lord Spencer was going. When I told him to leave me alone, he took it quite literally."

Barclay studied her for a moment.

Rebecca swallowed. Generally, she thought her features pleasing, with long, curly red hair and dark blue eyes. But she wasn't herself, and Barclay's presence made her jittery for a different set of reasons. He also didn't take her seriously, and this episode would strengthen that view. She was growing tired of being disrespected.

"Are you all right?" he asked quietly.

"I'll keep. I want to take a long, hot bath and forget today."

"Does something need to be done about the so-called gentleman?"

Her heart swelled. *He's responding with the seriousness this deserves.* "I punched him. That should be sufficient, though his jaw did a job on my fist."

Kenneth raised an eyebrow and then dismounted. "If you'll permit me to examine your hand and determine if you need a physician."

"I think it'll be fine, but you may." *If Lord Spencer messed it up for the hunt, I'll be fit to be tied.*

Kenneth turned her hand over in his. "Your knuckles are swollen, but as you said, it should heal. You appear to have full mobility."

Rebecca drew her hand towards her again, forcing the butterflies in her stomach to settle. It's not often she's in such close proximity to Barclay. *I'm reacting like a lovelorn schoolgirl, and I'm not in the mood for that sort of thing.*

"I thought you were cavorting with the gardener boy?" he asked. "Not that anyone believed it was going anywhere."

Rebecca glared at him. *When you're acquainted with someone since birth, they know too much and feel free to ask too many questions.* "Not anymore. I moved on." She frowned. "Or back, I suppose. The gardener treated me much better than this. He acted as a gentleman ought."

Barclay nodded. "I'll escort you home. Would you prefer to ride with me, or should we walk?"

"Riding would be better if your horse will put up with the both of us."

They rode in silence for a bit, Rebecca seated in front of Barclay as his horse walked at a slow gait.

Rebecca's tension eased from her. Barclay drove her mad for many reasons, but he wouldn't let anyone else hurt her.

"This is a long way to be somewhere unchaperoned," he commented.

Rebecca felt her back get up. *That tone of his.*

During the last two years, Barclay could find the perfect way to aggravate her, knowingly and in ignorance, as though it were his expertise. Apparently, this encounter wouldn't be any different. "I informed you, I didn't realize the direction the outing was taking," she retorted. "You may think me simple, but I'm not an idiot, and what happened wasn't my fault."

"I didn't mean to imply that," Barclay replied. "It was a thoughtless observation, and I apologize."

She exhaled. "Are you preparing the estate for your near marriage with Miss Hannah?" she asked, attempting a more conversational tone and change of subject, even though that question pained her.

"There'll be no marriage with Hannah," he responded tightly. "At least not with me."

What? Her heart galloped. "You two seemed positively smitten with one another."

Barclay's face was stone. "Things change."

The birds twittered in the trees as Rebecca trained her eyes on him. *Is Barclay free?*

"You're not smitten with her anymore?" she asked. "Or she's not smitten with you? That seems, unlike Miss Hannah—"

"I'd rather not discuss it right now."

Not exactly free, but he's not with Miss Hannah Northrop. "So it's quite fresh." Rebecca patted his hand. "I'm very sorry."

Despite her other feelings, she was sincere. There was no question Barclay had been besotted with Hannah.

His brown eyes softened. "Thank you."

Rebecca forgot herself and gazed at him.

He raised an eyebrow. "Do you have another question for me?"

She tore herself away. "Why are you here? To check on things for your father?"

"Laidley Park is mine. I have full control of it, so I'll be living here."

"Really?!" she squealed.

"Really," deadpanned Barclay.

"Finally, something new around here. I thought I'd die of boredom. And you'll certainly create a stir."

Rebecca was wild with excitement despite her general disinclination towards men at the moment. *Barclay will be here, and he's not with Hannah.*

Maybe now I have a shot.

✳✳✳✳✳

Rebecca tightened her grip on her pistol as the target came into range. Grasping the reins, she guided her horse, Mason, with one hand. *The key will be maintaining control once I shoot.* Rebecca took aim and pulled the trigger.

Mason jerked back, and Rebecca tugged on the reins to calm him. That took less effort now. Mason wasn't a skittish horse by nature, and he was slowly getting used to the sound of the gun.

"Not bad," called her father, Gregory Tarleton, Viscount of Eamon.

Rebecca smiled. *It must have been an excellent shot.*

It was Wednesday morning during the third week of October. The air was cool, and the sun hid in and out of the clouds. Rebecca and her father were on the elaborate shooting range at their home, Stoddard Grove, in Wiltshire. The house proper resembled a hunting mansion rather than a grand estate and was a touch countrified for some in their rank and status. But Rebecca knew and loved nothing else. It had been her and Papa since she was a baby.

Rebecca had her father's dark blue eyes, but that was where the physical likenesses ended. Lord Eamon was a robust blond man who wore his hair longer than the norm, usually tied back, and grew a beard. He reminded Rebecca of a physically fit warrior, but he carefully melded his rugged appearance with the elaborate dress of those in their station, creating an attention-getting presence.

"Your holster on the way I showed you?" Father had outfitted her with one for a small knife and pistol.

"Yes, Papa. I never ride without it." Yesterday's ordeal in the woods had been an exception, but then she'd thought the outing with her suitor would remain closer to estate grounds.

The forests here were tame with respect to fending off deadly creatures, but at least she could fashion shelter, a fire, and obtain food if necessary. Her father always impressed upon her a healthy respect for the land and animals. He insisted on hunting solely for food and striving for the cleanest and most accurate shot possible.

"It's only for the woods in case you get lost again," her father said. "It might be odd for you to be in company with it."

"If there were more company around that might be a larger problem."

"Speaking of company, I paid Lord Spencer a visit and made it clear I wouldn't be responsible for my actions if he ever laid hands on you again. I'll make his behavior known among my acquaintances."

"Thank you," Rebecca said quietly.

He peered at her. "I hope this helps some."

"Yes, this was very thoughtful."

It was empowering to engage in an activity in which she was an expert. She couldn't recall a time in her life when she wasn't upon some four-legged animal — pony, horse, even donkeys, mules, and camels in their travels. Her father had introduced her to archery at a young age, and then he'd switched her bows for guns. She liked the power of the guns, but she needed to respect it, like the forest beyond.

They rode their horses at a trot towards the stable.

"Do you know anything about Barclay's sudden appearance yesterday?" Rebecca asked.

"I was as surprised to see him as you, for I'd think his father would've informed me of such a development. Something considerable must have transpired."

"Barclay is no longer with Miss Northrop."

"I wasn't aware he was actually with her."

Rebecca snickered. "Whatever it was, Miss Northrop put a definitive end to it by courting another."

"That would explain some things," her father replied. "but Percival wouldn't give Kenneth Laidley Park to heal his bruised heart and ego. More must have occurred."

Depending on the circumstances of Miss Northrop's and Barclay's separation, Rebecca could see Barclay's father not wholly without compassion but stressing the need for him to deal with the turn of events and move forward.

Barclay didn't do that well.

Her father grinned. "Why don't you ask Kenneth yourself?"

Rebecca gave an unladylike snort. "As highly entertaining as that'd be, I'd annoy him more than I already do."

CHAPTER 2

Projects

Kenneth

Kenneth Barclay analyzed the ship's merchandise list on his desk. The vessel was nearly completed, and they were adding finishing touches and points of decoration. Preparing for his departure from Archer Hall at Putnam, his former home, and traveling to Laidley Park had left him behind schedule.

As he worked, he tried to ignore the sounds of activity outside his study. He'd sent an express to alert the staff of his arrival, but that still hadn't given them much time to prepare, so they were flurrying about. Typically, his father gave a couple of months' notice when they came, so everything was cleaned and fixed top to bottom, and the pantry was well stocked.

Kenneth stretched his tall and broad frame, pleased this desk had a large chair. Small, dainty chairs made him feel confined, and he deemed his existence hemmed in and common as it was — ordinary brown eyes, average light brown hair. He reckoned his looks good enough to be pleasant but not excite attention, his manners pleasing but not exceptional, and the same could be said for his intelligence. People described Kenneth as an agreeable gentleman, and while there was nothing wrong with that, it wasn't remarkable either, and that's where their descriptions ended. He needn't fame, but it'd be nice to have an identity.

The housekeeper entered. "Mr. Barclay, the pigs escaped their pen. All have been recovered, except one, and we're still searching for him."

"We have pigs?" Kenneth asked, surprised. He'd been keeping up with the affairs at Laidley Park for some time before his permanent arrival, and he didn't recall any matters concerning swine.

"Yes, sir. It was a pet project of your father's. He expressed an earnest desire for more ham and bacon when he visited."

"Do you require my assistance in the search?" He was perplexed why he needed to be informed of this in real time. *Surely they'll find the pig. It's not as though they sprint for long periods.*

"No, that's unnecessary," she replied. "We didn't want you alarmed in case you spotted one in the garden, fountain, or some other odd place."

"That would've been a sight." Kenneth grinned. "If that occurs, I'll let you know immediately."

She curtsied and left.

That was the type of information a steward would have given him if he had one. The one for Archer Hall had managed both properties, but it'd be appropriate for him to hire his own. Laidley Park was smaller than most country estates and passed into the Barclay family through his late stepmother.

Kenneth directed attention towards his papers again about the voyage to put his boat through moderate stress tests and ascertain its top speed. He wasn't wild about a winter journey and sailing during this political climate, but if he did so, the ship would be ready by spring, which would be suitable for Lord Spalding's first shipping run.

This project was one of the few things he had entirely of his own, and now he owned Laidley Park. Kenneth and his father rarely saw eye to eye, but it was sound judgment making him wait to take over the estate. Father had said he was ready.

It was time to put that declaration to the test.

CHAPTER 3

Familiarity Breeds Contempt

Rebecca

For a couple of hundred years, the Tarletons and their neighbors acquired meat for their households through the annual hunt safely and enjoyably. Papa continued the tradition, but the focus switched towards archery and other festivities to entertain, something akin to a gentlemen's house party. He still included a hunting component to provide meat for the estate, as he disliked it from the markets.

Rebecca offered to hand-deliver Barclay's invitation, though her father had planned on doing so to welcome him formally into the neighborhood. She hoped to ferret out the circumstances of his arrival in greater detail and ultimately sought an excuse to see Barclay in better dress and state than the day he had arrived.

Rebecca had liked Barclay since she was fifteen, and he was a young man of twenty. She had thought him the handsomest man of her acquaintance with his warm brown eyes and strong jawline, and at that time, the kindest as Barclay had treated her like a sister.

Her mind flashed back to when she'd first regarded him as a gentleman to fancy. Barclay had been in London all summer at the docks working with his boats and returned home sun-kissed. His skin was bronze, and his hair had streaks of gold in it. He also seemed hopeful and confident, like the water and his boats did him a world of good.

Barclay had seen her as a fifteen-year-old girl, as he properly should have, but that still disappointed her. Three years later, they began arguing constantly, and she entered society and courted other good-looking young men, but Barclay always held a special place in her heart. She missed the outdoorsy, happy, and carefree young man of that summer.

He'd never given Rebecca any encouragement, but she wanted to try for him since he was free again. Hence the dress dilemma — Rebecca bit her lip as she critically surveyed the two dresses hanging on her armoire door and selected the blue-gray one. It was a little somber and understated for her taste, but it became her well and was appropriate for the errand.

An hour later, the Tarleton's carriage pulled in front of Barclay's home, which was less than half a mile away from her own. Rebecca liked Laidley Park, for it was ideally situated and had the most appealing collection of trees and flowers with a pretty lane connecting their properties to the west. The main section of the home resembled a large, two-story cottage, and two substantial rectangular additions nestled both sides of the main chamber.

Rebecca was shown into the drawing room, where she admired the front gardens bursting with fall flowers from a large picture window.

A few minutes later, Barclay entered. "Rebecca, I didn't expect you to call."

"I have an invitation to deliver for my father's festivities in a few weeks."

Barclay took the invitation from her, and she strolled the room. "You like to live sparsely, I see."

"My arrival was unexpected. My things should be here in a few days."

"You rushed from Archer Hall?"

Sadness flashed in Barclay's eyes. "No time like the present to assume my responsibilities here."

I wish he'd think of me so deeply. "Miss Northrop's feelings changed?"

"What business is that of yours?"

"None. Merely a question. Is she still at Archer Hall?"

"You've not heard the news? Miss Northrop is an heiress and now Lady Corwyn, a countess in her own right."

Rebecca's jaw dropped as Barclay related the events. "I'm surprised my father hasn't heard from yours about these developments."

"The events transpired quickly and were of a delicate nature. I'm sure he'll receive a letter shortly. Are you acquainted with Lord Vaughnryd?"

"I am," Rebecca replied carefully. They'd been introduced two years ago when she and her father had toured the lake areas.

"Lady Corwyn is courting him." Barclay paced the room. "What did you think of him?"

Lord Vaughnryd had struck her as every inch the gentleman, with a bit of daring and a great deal of confidence and ability. "I found him very pleasing."

Barclay grunted. "Of course you did. Rich, handsome, charming Lord Vaughnryd with a large estate. Is that all young ladies see?"

"Of course not!" she snapped. "Don't blame this on Miss Northrop. She was yours. How did you boggle that?

Barclay wrenched the drawing room door open and stalked out of the room.

The butler ran in and apologetically showed her out.

I might have been harsh, but that was absolutely rude. Rebecca climbed into her carriage, seething. *Dismissed. I'm not a silly little girl anymore; I'm a woman of twenty with means. Perhaps it's time to get over my ridiculous interest in Barclay and move on to someone else.*

*****

Kenneth

Kenneth slammed into his chair in the study and rubbed his face. *Rebecca is infuriating, and even more so because she looked exceedingly well. She ruined what could have been a fine visit with all her questions.*

He was pleased to receive the invitation, and it gratified him that Rebecca was the one who delivered it. At least he'd been happy until she freely expressed her opinions and interrogated him.

Kenneth tried to resume his correspondence about the test voyage route and small sailing crew they'd have, but his concentration was shot to pieces. *I shouldn't have left Rebecca in the drawing room, no matter how familiar our acquaintance is.*

Their age disparity was wide enough for him to consider her a baby or child to his older age, but the maturity gap had diminished, and she grew into a beauty. Kenneth had difficulty viewing her as an adult, so it aggravated him to find her attractive. That switch happened about two years ago, and he'd been fighting it and her ever since.

Rebecca was having an increasingly absorbing effect on him that only Hannah had broken. Even then, there were moments, however few and far between, when Rebecca had unwittingly stolen his attention during her visit to Archer Hall this past spring.

I'll call on her tomorrow and apologize for my rudeness. But for now, a ride will clear my mind. He enjoyed riding at Putnam but loved it here because the scenery was more idyllic.

He'd been out for a bit when he crossed ways with Mr. Nash Repington, a distant relative of the Tarletons who lived nearby and would inherit a barony. Mr. Repington had the family's signature dark-blue eyes and a head of black hair that constantly fell in his eyes. Kenneth was well acquainted with him, as the two men were the same age.

"Barclay!" Repington exclaimed. "Are you up for Lord Eamon's festivities already?"

"I'll be attending," Kenneth replied. "But I've also assumed control of Laidley Park, so I live in the neighborhood now."

"Excellent! We can use some new blood around here."

"Rebecca had said as much. It can't be that dull."

"There aren't many younger ones residing here, so it's much quieter than it used to be," Repington explained. "Are you readying the place in preparation for a switch in status?"

Kenneth inwardly cringed. "Not at present. This is primarily a welcome change."

Repington studied him. "You're living next door to an eligible lady."

"I just rudely walked out on her after having another one of our regular arguments."

"Already? You couldn't have been here more than a week."

"Three days."

"You have a unique relationship with Miss Rebecca, for she's quite friendly with everyone else."

That observation was an additional reason Kenneth was annoyed they always argued. It was like she pushed and pulled all the right levers to make him explode.

Repington chuckled. "She's not even here, and you're growing agitated."

"We know one another too well. What's the expression? Familiarity breeds contempt?"

"Your familiarity could easily head in the opposite direction."

"Impossible."

Repington still seemed amused. "That's my relation you're talking about, and Rebecca and I are actually friends."

Kenneth winced. "I apologize. It's not that I think badly of her."

"No offense taken." Repington was still smiling. "I wish to stay on Lord Eamon's good side, and bashing his beloved daughter would be counterproductive. However, you've remained in his good graces despite the fighting. He must greatly favor you."

"I doubt it," Kenneth muttered. He wondered if Lord Eamon regarded him as something of a joke, for his father's friend always teased him.

The two men chatted for a while and then parted.

Kenneth felt like he was closer to making this place his home. But he had imagined he'd be here with a wife and family.

CHAPTER 4

The Apology

Rebecca

Rebecca spent the morning going over arrangements for the hunt with the house staff and afterward amused herself by playing darts in the gentlemen's room. In time, the butler informed her Mr. Barclay was in the drawing room to call upon her.

Rebecca froze. *Barclay? Calling on me?*

It was proper calling hours, and had she been in the habit of receiving visitors, she would've dressed appropriately. Rebecca tossed her apron in the corner, grimacing at her reflection in the mirror. Her garb and hair arrangement were rather youthful. *Let's see what Barclay wants. It's probably something to do with the hunt, though I can't imagine why he wouldn't ask to see Papa.*

The drawing room was pleasant enough but seldom used and light of furnishings, as her father preferred entertaining in the great room. The furniture was in good repair, but the setting had remained much as it was when great-grandmother Lady Eamon originally insisted on building a respectable drawing room.

Rebecca entered and almost staggered. *Good gracious, Barclay looks outstanding, as though he carefully chose his attire for this visit.* She dropped into a curtsy. "What can I do for you?"

"Thank you for receiving me," he replied. "I came to apologize for my boorish behavior yesterday. It was inconsiderate to walk out on you as I did."

Rebecca had no notion he'd make a special trip to apologize; he could've done so the next time they were together. "Thank you. It was kind of you to come expressly for that purpose."

For the first time in their acquaintance, Rebecca felt awkward with Barclay as they stood quietly together. Despite her interest, she'd always been at ease with him as during childhood.

This visit didn't feel like childhood anymore.

"Would you like to stay for tea?" she asked him.

"Certainly. Thank you."

They took seats, and Rebecca searched for generalities to chat about — another uncommon dilemma. Subjects of discussion usually came readily to mind and frequently deteriorated into arguments.

"How are you settling in?" she inquired.

"Well. How are the hunt preparations coming along?"

"Nicely. I worked with the servants to ensure all the guests will be comfortable."

The housekeeper brought refreshments, and Rebecca poured them tea and offered spice bread. They ate and drank in silence for a bit.

This is very proper, and I appreciate Barclay engaging me in such an adult manner, but it's too sedate. Is this what entertaining like a lady is supposed to be like? "How did you spend your morning?"

He chuckled. "Wrestling a pig."

Rebecca was taken aback for a second and then laughed. "I'm sure there are other ways to amuse yourself until your things arrive."

He joined her in laughter. "This was quite an accident. Lately, the pigs have made a game of breaking out of the pen. While on my walk, one waddled in front of me, easy as you please, and I decided to help the staff catch it."

"Did you succeed?"

"The pig and I both ended up in one of the flower beds. He happily, me less so. And the gardener was decidedly put out as we made a mess of his winter daffodils and dahlias."

Rebecca giggled.

"The pigs don't move fast, but I had the hardest time coaxing him in the direction I wished, and he definitely didn't appreciate being pushed or held," Barclay continued. "But I won in the end."

"It almost sounds like fun."

"There might be one or two still roaming if you'd like to try your hand at it. I wouldn't mind another opportunity. The pig would probably be no match against the two of us."

Rebecca jumped up. "I'm game. Let's get some pigs."

Barclay set his teacup down, and the two made their way towards the door.

Papa entered the room. "Afternoon Kenneth, leaving already?"

"Yes," Barclay replied. "I apologize for departing so abruptly, but Rebecca said she'd help me catch a couple of pigs. You're welcome to join us if you wish."

Lord Eamon glanced between them and laughed. "No, thank you, I'll leave the pig chasing to the two of you." He left the room, still chuckling.

*****

Rebecca and Barclay stood on the front lawn of Laidley Park.

"The pig I came across was on the side of the house." Barclay walked towards a small stone pond containing goldfish with flower beds on either side.

They heard a commotion, and then two pigs ran across the lawn, followed by a couple of servants in pursuit.

Rebecca took off with Barclay on her heels.

"Milady, we can take care of this," a servant called.

"It's fine," Barclay assured her. "I invited her here for this very task."

The servant girl gave him an odd glance as they all came to a stop.

"We're assisting," Kenneth explained.

"With all due respect, sir, might you recall the dahlia incident," the older servant ventured.

"The event has been named," Rebecca remarked. "Marvelous way to begin your tenure here, Barclay."

"The gardener was sputtering," the servant girl told Rebecca with great significance.

"Mr. Barclay frequently has that effect on me as well," Rebecca replied. "Perhaps I should find the poor man and commiserate."

Barclay made a face. "I apologized to you."

"And I appreciated it. Did you apologize to the gardener for ruining all his hard work?" Rebecca teased.

"I did, but they're my dahlias. If I wish to roll around and play in them, I should be free to do so without reference to anyone else," Barclay declared. "Pig included."

"Quite correct, sir."

"I'll keep Mr. Barclay with me and make sure any ensuing swine battles remain contained," Rebecca said.

"The flowers will grow back," Barclay insisted.

"Indeed," agreed the older servant. "But any battle plan will be strictly moot if the pigs leave the county while we're discussing it."

They turned their attention to the matter at hand as two more hired workers ran towards them.

Rebecca, Barclay, and the servant girl blocked the pigs' path. The swine made sounds of protest but turned from the pond.

"To where are we leading them?" Rebecca asked as she slowed down.

Maybe firm and gentle guidance would do the trick. They were rather cute, not large, and light pink with flippy ears.

Barclay pointed. "We keep the livestock about a quarter-mile north of here. It's penned in to maintain cleanliness and some appearance of organization, though clearly, you can see we have no control at present."

Rebecca chuckled as they spotted a third one sitting under a tree.

"Rebecca and I can corral the third one if the rest of you could continue with these two," Barclay said.

"Mr. Barclay—" the hired man pulled off his hat and scratched his head.

"It's fine," Barclay reassured him.

He and Rebecca coaxed the third one towards the barn, but it took a while because the pig wanted to go touring. By the time they'd arrived, the others had just gotten their pigs into the proper area. Everything was secured as much as possible, and the servants rushed away, for now they were behind on the day's chores.

Rebecca and Barclay collapsed against each other on a nearby bale of hay, exchanged looks, and then began laughing hysterically.

"If anyone had seen us like that—" Rebecca began.

"We'd be dismissed from polite society," Barclay finished.

Rebecca's mirth vanished. She was sitting with a gentleman on this dirty bale of hay after chasing pigs back into the barn. *What was I doing?*

"That was in jest," Barclay said. "They'd have to find out first, and I don't plan on divulging that information to anyone."

"You told me."

"That's different." He grinned at her. "This will have to be our little secret. Well, ours and my entire servant staff."

Rebecca smiled back at him.

The two sat in silence, still leaning upon one another.

"I wish we didn't fight so much," Barclay said. "We should have afternoons like this more often."

"Chasing pigs and tromping through the mud? I'm sure you wouldn't do that with any other lady."

"No, I wouldn't. I can't seem to be me with any other lady but you. Much to your great consternation, I'd imagine."

"Not at all, I assure you." *He's all I ever really wanted. I wish I dared to speak plainly.*

He stood and pulled her up from the bale of hay. "I suppose you'd wish to get back home now. Unless you'd like to stay for supper."

Rebecca peered at him for a moment. That invitation seemed very personal. "I thank you, but I'm not really fit for company."

He grinned. "I'm company now? I must have risen in your estimation."

"You must be company like no other, for I wouldn't chase pigs with any other gentleman."

Barclay sobered, and still holding her hands, leaned over and kissed her. He pulled away and leaned his forehead against hers.

I can't believe this is happening. Rebecca would love nothing more than to have this moment with him for eternity, but the hour was getting late. She stepped back. "I should leave," she said quietly.

Her words seemed to break him from a trance, and he dropped her hands. "Of course, thank you for your assistance."

Rebecca was having a hard time reading him. "You're very welcome."

They stared at one another for a second longer, and then Rebecca fled Laidley Park.

Barclay, you're creating a stir already.

*****

Kenneth

Kenneth lay in bed that night, wide awake.

He was supposed to apologize like a gentleman, not wrestle pigs with Rebecca Tarleton. And then he'd completely lost his mind and kissed her. *What was I thinking? She had a bad experience a few weeks ago, and that man was her suitor. I'm fortunate she was polite and amicable towards me.*

He didn't expect a visit to apologize to be pleasant, but his nervousness around Rebecca when he first arrived at Stoddard Grove was peculiar. Perhaps it was her appearance, as she was lovely. She seemed comfortable and one with her surroundings and home, and Kenneth liked that immensely.

That was probably why he issued the inane invitation to chase pigs with him. At the time, it sounded like an appealing and diverting way to keep Rebecca in his company longer. In hindsight, it was an absurd request.

I can't court her. It'd feel odd. I've known her forever and have always seen her as a little girl.

Until he didn't, and that made a mess of his mind.

Rebecca certainly wouldn't want it, considering the men she'd courted in the last couple of years. Most of them were good-looking, rich, and charismatic, like Lord Vaughnryd.

If I don't plan on courting Rebecca, then I have no business kissing her.

He rolled over as a deep sense of longing and disappointment overtook him.

CHAPTER 5

Lady Jocelyn Arrives

Rebecca

The wind whipped Rebecca's dress as she pulled her shawl tighter, feeling the dampness in her bones. Papa stood beside her as Lady Jocelyn Grayson's carriage turned into the side entrance. They frequently received guests here since the front door opened directly into their great room. Sometimes that was inviting, but other times Rebecca wished for a more formal front receiving area. The side was well landscaped, with an attractive balustrade and terrace, but it was still odd. Their house had the trappings of other fashionable country homes, but the spaces were situated differently since it'd been built as a hunting lodge. The Tarleton men liked to keep it that way, though it was now a full-fledged estate and residence.

Lady Jocelyn was the only daughter of a wealthy widower earl, and she'd been a diverting companion during the weeks Rebecca was in London after she and Papa visited Archer Hall. Rebecca had thrown herself into the social scene, and it had distracted her from thoughts of Hannah and Barclay courting and marrying, though that had never materialized. She had been incredibly conflicted because she liked Hannah a great deal and had befriended her during that visit.

Lady Jocelyn stepped out of the carriage, holding her hat as a gust of wind threatened to dislodge it.

"How wonderful to see you again!" Rebecca exclaimed.

She gave Rebecca a faux peck on the cheek. "It's marvelous to be with you, Miss Tarleton."

Lady Jocelyn possessed captivating features — dark brown hair, upturned eyes of the same color, and high cheekbones. She dressed in the latest fashions, always said the right thing, and was confident without appearing unladylike.

That was a trait Rebecca would like to gain. Her forthrightness made her appear a little uncouth. Not horribly so, but she fit the Tarleton reputation of being a touch too rustic.

"Welcome to Stoddard Grove," her father said. "Pull out a chair and throw up your feet. We don't act on ceremony around here."

"Papa," Rebecca said, exasperated. *We can act with a little more ceremony since Lady Jocelyn is here.*

"It won't get any better once the gentlemen arrive. She might as well grow accustomed to it now."

Rebecca wasn't ashamed of her home and the manner in which she'd been raised, but she would like to become more genteel. In her heart of hearts, she was afraid that in never having a mother, she wouldn't know how to act like a proper woman of her station. Being a hostess for the next couple of weeks should be good practice.

"I'm sure Rebecca will tend to your every care while you're here, Lady Jocelyn. Enjoy your stay."

"Thank you, Lord Eamon. I believe I shall."

"Let's go inside before we get blown away," Rebecca said.

A month ago, Lady Jocelyn had written complaining that the man she was courting, Lord Manton, wasn't paying her attention. Rebecca suggested she visit Stoddard Grove during the hunting party, and wouldn't the company she'd keep make her beau wild with envy? Lady Jocelyn loved the idea and readily accepted. Though Rebecca would be an active participant in her father's festivities, some female companionship would be welcome. The wives rarely accompanied their husbands, and Rebecca hadn't heard of any planning to do so this year.

Rebecca showed Lady Jocelyn to the room in which she'd be staying. "It's smaller than you're accustomed to, but I think it should be comfortable."

Lady Jocelyn laid her hat on the bed. "This is very quaint and pretty. Thank you."

Quaint. I'm not sure if that's good or bad. "You must tell me about this courtship," Rebecca said as the girls entered the drawing room.

Lady Jocelyn daintily dropped onto the couch. "It's been awful. He never has time for me anymore. I might as well not exist."

"I'm surprised he's inattentive now. He was so pleasing in London."

Lady Jocelyn usually had the problem of too many men paying her too much attention. She'd met Lord Manton this past spring in London, and they made a splendid couple in appearance and manner. He would be a duke with an impressive estate one day, and Rebecca thought him a phenomenal catch.

"That's how they get you," Lady Jocelyn declared. "Though none were as bad as my first courtship. He was so controlling."

"How long ago was that?"

"I'm twenty-three now, so I suppose it was as much as seven or eight years ago."

Rebecca's eyes grew wide. "You were rather young. Was he a childhood sweetheart?"

Lady Jocelyn snorted. "No, my dear. I never had one of those. I met him while I was away at school. He was twenty-five and had no plans to marry me, so he had to go. And when he became more insistent, shall we say, Papa had to step in."

"I'm surprised he didn't step in sooner."

"I'm rather good at hiding things."

Rebecca couldn't imagine hiding something so important from her father. *The man sounds like a Lord Spencer, though we were closer in age.* "I've had my own terrible experiences with men I met in London."

They shared accounts of their awful courtship partners until the butler informed them dinner would be at five o'clock, and Mr. Barclay would dine with them.

Rebecca's mouth went a little dry as she played with a strand of hair, recalling his visit a couple of weeks prior and the subsequent barn affair. She hadn't seen or heard from him since. That didn't surprise her, but it was frustrating. She predicted he'd have some mixed feelings, but an indication as to which way he was leaning or what he was thinking would've been appreciated. The silence was maddening.

The girls headed for their rooms to prepare since it was already after four.

"Who's Mr. Barclay?" Lady Jocelyn asked. "A friend of your father's?"

"He's the son of my father's closest friend," Rebecca replied. "Are you acquainted with the Barclays of Archer Hall at Putnam?"

"Not personally. My father is acquainted with Lord Putnam, and he seems quite formidable. Is his son like him?"

Rebecca chuckled. "Not at all."

*****

Lord Eamon was quite wealthy, and over the last couple of years, Rebecca had put some of that wealth to use by expanding her wardrobe with eye-catching dresses and jewelry. She also had her own sizeable nest egg, left by her mother and in her father's care until she turned twenty-one the following year. Rebecca wanted the respect her station and income should afford her and wished to marry in a way that would allow her to continue that lifestyle. In anticipation of seeing Barclay, she chose her dinner attire more carefully than she ordinarily would. She donned a red dress saved for special occasions when she wanted to stand out.

An hour later, Lady Jocelyn wasn't ready, so Rebecca went downstairs ahead of her.

Barclay had been received into the house seconds before, brushing rain off his person and coat.

"Rebecca, good," he said anxiously. "We need to speak."

"Why don't you follow me to the morning room?"

Rebecca spent a fair number of her daytime hours in the morning room when she wasn't outside. Her father was seldom in there, and it was unlikely that Lady Jocelyn would wander in, so it would serve as a fitting place for a private interview. Rebecca shut the door after them.

"About the last time we saw one another..." Barclay faltered. "We can't do that."

Pain shot through her chest as she crossed her arms. *That was pathetic.* "You were the one who initiated it."

"Yes, I'm sorry—"

"You're apologizing?"

"I shouldn't kiss a woman I'm not courting and don't plan on courting," he said in a lowered voice.

"I see," Rebecca said tightly. "So it was a mistake in your eyes?"

"The word mistake sounds severe."

"And declaring you have no desire to be my suitor isn't?"

"You want me to actually court you?" Barclay asked incredulously.

"You make it sound as though it were a fate worse than death."

"Because we'd kill each other inside of a week. I can't court you."

"Why not? Other than the death thing."

"Because you're—" He waved a hand around. "You."

Rebecca's jaw dropped like her body temperature, and then it shot straight to boiling.

"That sounded worse than I meant it." Barclay retreated.

"But I understood your full meaning." Rebecca flung the door open and marched through it.

"No, you don't." Kenneth rushed after her. "I didn't mean your whole person was disagreeable—"

"Merely most of it."

"As if you never mocked or poked fun at me—"

Her father entered the corridor. "Kenneth! I didn't know you had arrived already."

Rebecca and Barclay stopped short.

Barclay plastered on a smile. "Yes, Lord Eamon, just."

The three stood in silence.

"I'm pleased Rebecca was available to see to your comfort, though the morning room is usually her special space," her father said.

Barclay glanced at her. "We had something sensitive to discuss."

Rebecca snorted. "Don't be timid, Barclay. Why don't you share with Father what we were debating?"

Barclay's glower could've incinerated her. "And you wonder why I said what I did?"

"I don't want to know." Lord Eamon chuckled. "Let's get down to the business of eating, shall we?"

Lady Jocelyn joined them, and a few minutes later, the four were seated around the dinner table. When it was only Rebecca and her father, they ate in the great room, but the dining room was used for company.

Barclay discussed the final phase of his shipbuilding and the voyage he must take before finalizing the agreement with Lord Spalding.

That journey could be an exciting adventure. "I'd like to go too," Rebecca chimed in.

Barclay stared at her as though she'd grown another head.

Rebecca was astonished she'd voiced that wish aloud too. Few young ladies would sail at this time unless absolutely necessary, and after the insanity of the last conversation, spending any length of time with Barclay should be anathema.

Amazingly, it wasn't.

Now that it's out, let's see where it leads. "I'm in earnest."

"I can't take you on a ship testing journey," Barclay replied. "The safety of the craft isn't guaranteed."

Rebecca smirked. "You doubt your own vessel?"

He scowled at her. "No. But it's common sense not to take a lady on such a voyage. Notwithstanding

the state of battle this country is in and the profusion
of smugglers right now, I'm not a fan of sailing with
ladies, period."

"Why ever not?"

"It's impossible to make the accommodations necessary to keep them comfortable."

"Maybe the ladies of your acquaintance. I don't
require all the extra trappings."

"I did say ladies," Barclay retorted. "A girl such as
yourself who's next door to a complete wild woman
could happily make herself at home perched upon the
mast."

"And you're such the gentleman to strap me
there," Rebecca fired back.

Her father chortled. "You two are ridiculous."

"I propose a deal," Rebecca said, struggling for
composure. "If I win the hunt—"

"You're participating in the hunt?" Barclay asked
derisively.

She gritted her teeth. *Why do I like this man?*

"I told you before, she's as good as any man I hunt
with," her father said. "Now you'll witness it with your
own eyes."

Barclay appeared skeptical but said nothing further.

"If I beat you in the hunt," she began again, sup-
pressing a growl, "then you have to take Lady Jocelyn
and me with you on the sailing test." Not that she'd
consulted Lady Jocelyn at all, but Rebecca thought she
might be agreeable.

"And if I win?" Barclay asked with a cocky air.

Rebecca narrowed her eyes. *I'll show you a thing or
two, no matter how well you wear that smirk.* "I'll invest in
your next shipbuilding project."

CHAPTER 6

The Deal

Kenneth

The woman is mad.

Kenneth opened his mouth to give another searing reply and then snapped it shut. *An investment in my next project would be useful, especially from a party so near to me.*

"You possess the means?" he asked. "This isn't like buying several dresses from the mercantile."

Rebecca glared at him.

Kenneth fought another wave of frustration. *I don't wish to insult and be rude, but I can't see her as a grown woman yet. She's simply...*

Rebecca.

He shifted in his seat.

At first, he'd been relieved to intercept her privately before dinner, but that conversation had turned into a disaster. *Why did I think it'd be anything different?*

"My mother left money that has been accumulating a hefty amount of interest for me over the years untouched." Rebecca narrowed her eyes further. "I have the funds."

Kenneth swallowed, because she looked highly appealing at that moment. *That's what landed me in trouble in the first place.* "No. All my original objections still stand."

Lady Jocelyn took a sip of wine. "While a sailing journey sounds exciting, it's good of you to watch over our comfort and safety in such a fastidious manner, Mr. Barclay."

"Thank you." Kenneth smirked at Rebecca as she gaped at her friend. "Rebecca is fortunate to have such a reasonable friend as yourself."

Lady Jocelyn raised an eyebrow. "We may be friends, but it appears you're very close to Miss Tarleton to refer to her in such a bold manner."

Kenneth winced. "I've known Miss Tarleton since she was a little girl, but you're correct in that I need not be forward with her in public."

"And when you're not?" Lady Jocelyn asked.

Rebecca shot him an arch look.

Kenneth returned it. "All bets are off."

Her gaze grew too intense for him, and he grabbed his glass and took a swig. *I could use a strong drink with Lord Eamon right about now.*

*****

Rebecca

After dinner, Rebecca attempted to settle herself as the two women walked back to the drawing room. *Barclay will turn me into a basket case, always winding me up like a top. I'm supposed to be acting well-bred and elegant.*

Lady Jocelyn beamed. "You're absolutely brilliant!"

"How so?" Rebecca replied, perplexed.

"Making my so-called beau pay attention to me by coming here. Mr. Barclay might be exactly the man to force him to take notice."

Rebecca pressed her lips together. She should've seen this coming or at least been aware of the possibility. After the row Barclay and Rebecca had, it wasn't difficult for Lady Jocelyn to set herself up as an agreeable alternative, and it was evident Barclay had enjoyed her attention the remainder of dinner.

"You didn't actually have hopes for him yourself, did you?" Lady Jocelyn asked as she sat on the couch again.

Rebecca fought a frown. *The idea isn't preposterous.* Lady Jocelyn asked like it was a ridiculous notion for her to entertain. Rebecca didn't want to share the pig chase and barn affair with her friend. She feared doing so would somehow tarnish how special that afternoon was because Lady Jocelyn wouldn't understand.

"I don't like the idea of using him," Rebecca replied. "He recently had a romantic difficulty. It'd be cruel for me to allow him to get into another situation where I know he'll be disappointed again."

"But it would've been fine for one of the other gentlemen?"

Rebecca cringed. "I should've thought out my suggestion more thoroughly."

"Don't worry. I'm not completely without heart. I find Mr. Barclay agreeable, and he is handsome. If he plays his cards right, he may sway me." Lady Jocelyn stretched. "Do you mind if I retire early? I'm quite fatigued."

"No, of course not. You must be exhausted from your journey."

They said goodnight, and Rebecca remained in the drawing room, hoping the silence would soothe her agitation. *I wish I didn't have hopes for Barclay, as it seems to provide more vexation than anything. He made it clear he has no intentions of pursuing any type of attachment with me.*

Rebecca's stomach dropped as she relived the look they shared at dinner. Despite his words earlier in the morning room, that instant seemed to hold a promise that their freeness could unfold into something greater.

It already has, whether or not he wants to admit it. Restless, Rebecca headed to the library.

Her father smiled indulgently from the table. "Daughter, what brings you here? I'd thought you'd want to catch up with Lady Jocelyn."

"She was exhausted from her journey and wished to retire early. Are you working on plans for the hunt?"

"Aye, would you like to assist me?"

"Sure."

The library was used for projects as opposed to a place for housing literature and reading. Their selection of books was small and mostly reference and language materials, as they had little fiction. The room featured a massive oak table, mementos and treasures from their journeys, and other implements and tools to help build contraptions.

This year's event was a competition with various challenges. Her father had split the guests into two teams. Each guest would compete as an individual, and the two teams would compete against each other.

Rebecca's heart thudded as she scanned the lists. "Barclay and I are on the same team?"

"I thought I'd liven things up with extra side entertainment."

Rebecca gave him a look.

"This will make your deal more exciting," he continued. "The two of you will have to work together as a team and simultaneously try to defeat one another for the deal." His dark blue eyes twinkled. "You'll bring him up to your level and then knock him down again. It'll be so diverting to watch."

Rebecca shook her head. *Father is always scheming.* "He never agreed to the deal."

"I have a feeling he'll change his mind once the others arrive." He winked at her. "Now help me with this catapult design. Things aren't flying as far as I need them to."

Rebecca groaned. "Papa, do we really need a catapult?"

"Of course. How else will we have a moving target challenge?"

"I'll be a laughingstock."

Her father made an odd noise. "Forget them. It's especially amusing when they're shocked and appalled at our diversions."

"I like society, Papa. I rather not shock them."

"You're fine, and make sure any gentleman going after you knows that. No more Lord Spencers. It was fortunate Kenneth was there to do you right." He suddenly seemed despondent. "Your mother and I used to do archery all the time when we courted. I'm proud you took to it as well as you did. At least I did that right."

"Whatever do you mean, Papa?"

"Never you mind; it's not important now."

Rebecca's parents had been childhood sweethearts and married at a young age, but her mother passed away during childbirth. Papa had remarried, and his second wife had also lost her life giving birth to a son who died a few weeks later. At present, he didn't appear to be in any hurry to marry a third time.

"You and Kenneth are a bit like your mother and me," Papa said.

"Barclay doesn't see me in that way."

Her father regarded her. "Do you want him to?"

Rebecca flushed. "No girl wants to be ignored by a handsome nobleman."

Her father chuckled. "I wouldn't say Barclay ignores you."

"Arguing with me constantly, calling me a child, and treating me accordingly is not caring for me."

"He may be much closer than either of you realize and probably knows you better than most."

I'm not sure that last comment makes me feel any better. "You think his treatment is warranted?"

"Of course not. But I doubt it's as negative as you believe it is, though I understand the irritation."

"It's just as well. I'm sure he seeks a more ladylike wife."

"You're a lady."

"You're hopeless. You know how esteemed ladies act."

Her father frowned. "I'm glad you're doing this competition. You need a reminder of who you are and how good that is."

"You have to say that because you're my father."

"I say it because it's true. Being your father doesn't have to have much to do with it. Consider Percival with Kenneth."

"Well, yes. They have an odd father-son relationship, but then Lord Putnam is a singular man."

"He is that. So are you to help me with this catapult?"

Rebecca laughed. "I give up. What would you like me to do?"

CHAPTER 7

Leap In

Kenneth

Percival Barclay, the Earl of Putnam, opted to lodge at Laidley Park with Kenneth during the festivities. Though Stoddard Grove could accommodate everyone attending, Lord Eamon thought the guests would be more comfortable spread between the two residences and asked the Barclays if they'd be willing to take another gentleman, Mr. Luke Notley.

Kenneth had grown up with Mr. Notley and was happy to have him stay. He lived not too far from Archer Hall and was the son of a man with a moderately sized estate. Kenneth's father and Notley traveled to Laidley Park together and arrived two days before the official beginning of the hunt.

Lord Eamon stood next to Kenneth as they waited outside for the carriage to pull to a halt. The viscount was eager to welcome Lord Putnam, while Kenneth was more anxious, as he felt his father constantly found him wanting.

Kenneth's relationship with his father had turned contentious after Mama died. Giving him Laidley Park was a significant gesture in turning over a new leaf, and Kenneth hoped they'd continue deepening that altered understanding. He would live here until his father died and then become Viscount of Putnam. However, his father seemed immortal, and Kenneth preferred Laidley Park to Archer Hall. Other than the idea of having an early demise, he had no problems with his father outliving him.

"Percival!" Lord Eamon exclaimed as his father alighted from the carriage with a rare, bright smile.

As the two old friends exchanged warm greetings, Kenneth was briefly reminded of how his cantankerous father managed to have a best mate and marry two beautiful women, both dead now.

Notley hopped out of the carriage. "It's good to be out from there."

He was a slender fellow with light brown eyes, fine reddish-blond hair, and a complexion that quickly burned in the sun. Notley's features and a smattering of freckles across his nose lent him a boyish countenance.

"We can take a walk if you wish. Stretch your legs," said Kenneth. "Welcome to Laidley Park."

"Thank you, a walk in a bit sounds good," replied Notley. "But you can visit with your father. He was eager to spend time with you."

Eager might be stretching it.

His father stood beside him. Kenneth possessed his frame, but Father's hair was darker brown with streaks of gray at the temples, and his eyes were a piercing gray.

"The place looks good. At least you got all the pigs back." Father chuckled. "But if that's your largest problem, you're doing well."

The four of them entered the house, and Notley opted to take a short nap. Kenneth led his father and Lord Eamon into the drawing room.

"The pigs were a nice surprise," Kenneth commented dryly. "Any other secrets you want to clue me in on, Father?"

"I figured you'd like that one. You can thank me when you're gnawing on your bacon in the morning."

"How are the girls?" Kenneth asked.

His father shrugged. "Essentially, as you left them." He paused. "They leave by week's end to visit Hannah." Father briefly described the circumstances of the elder sister's courtship and his research into schools for the younger.

"You've been holding out on me, Percival," said Lord Eamon.

"My children seem to be taking life by the horns. There was little time to write, and events were in a constant state of flux." He smirked at Kenneth. "Ready to get your backside handed to you in this hunt?"

Kenneth tossed him a brassy grin. "I'm ready to beat you, old man."

His father threw his head back and laughed. "Kenneth, I do believe this move was good for you. I'll enjoy the hunt more this year in your company."

That's the kindest thing he's said to me in a long time. "I too."

"Do you think some bacon can be roused up for us now?" Lord Eamon asked. "Or some bread and good, strong cheese?"

"That can be arranged," Kenneth replied.

*****

Kenneth brought Notley up to speed on the happenings of the last six months during their walk later that afternoon, leaving out what had transpired between him and Rebecca.

"Take advantage of this hunt to relax," Notley said. "With no ladies around, it'd be good to let your hair down and recoup."

There'll be no recouping with Rebecca in the mix. She turns me inside out more than my situation with Hannah did. "Miss Tarleton and Lady Jocelyn will be present."

"Who's Lady Jocelyn?"

"A friend of Miss Tarleton's who's come to visit."

"Have you met her? What is she like?"

"Beautiful woman, pleasing manner. I enjoyed her company."

"Enjoyed as in you'd like to further the acquaintance?"

"I thought you were advising me to take a break from women and let my hair down."

"I was, but if you're ready to get back in the fray, by all means, leap in."

Kenneth chuckled. "I hadn't thought about becoming better acquainted with Lady Jocelyn. Her company was merely more pleasant than Miss Tarleton's."

"That's surprising. I've always found Miss Tarleton's company very agreeable."

"You're the second young man to say that to me in recent history. I don't understand why she's disagreeable only with me."

She has good reason now, but that doesn't explain before the pig chase.

Kenneth's natural inclination was to do as Notley had first suggested and enjoy the hunt with the company of the men here. But Lady Jocelyn was rather dazzling. *There's no harm in getting to know her better, is there? She'd be a good distraction from Rebecca, and tomorrow evening will be an excellent opportunity to do so.*

CHAPTER 8

Goaded

Kenneth

The following afternoon, Kenneth, his father, and Notley were shown into the great room at Stoddard Grove for Lord Eamon's dinner party to kick off the festivities. Stoddard Grove's great room was unlike any Kenneth had seen for its sheer size and simplistic country interior. Every activity in the house could occur in the great room — eating, socializing, games, studying. The window seat was substantial enough to be a bed if desired, and the massive fireplace resembled a hearth that could be cooked in.

The room was the length of the house, and the front door opened into it. The cheery yellow walls were lined with windows intermixed with large landscape paintings and family portraits. Drinks and small edibles had been arranged on two sideboards and a dining table. A fire was roaring, with a couple of over-sized upholstered chairs and a couch surrounding it. The space was a comfortable and inviting reprieve from the rainy weather outdoors.

Repington and Mr. Morgan Baxter played cards at the far end of the room near the billiards table. Smaller in stature, with a distinguished mustache and beard, Mr. Baxter was a wealthy gentleman with an estate in the neighborhood and often accompanied Lords Eamon and Putnam on their trips. Baxter was a married man, Kenneth's age, and his wife had given birth to a daughter last year.

Lord Spalding walked into the room, a pleasant-looking man with brown hair and gray eyes, and greeted the crowd with a boisterous hello.

Kenneth gave him a hearty handshake. "I'd no idea you'd be here."

"I'm not skilled enough to hunt for food like my brother, but I can do archery." Lord Spalding introduced Kenneth to his younger brother, Mr. Geoffrey Fitzpatrick.

They chatted about how each became acquainted with Lord Eamon.

"My father always lamented I was a bit soft, and Eamon roughened me up," Lord Spalding said. "He feels like an older brother to me." He excused himself so he could greet the host himself.

Kenneth turned towards Mr. Fitzpatrick, a gentleman with blond hair, green eyes, and striking features. "It sounds like you'll be stiff competition."

"Shooting was one of the few ways I could distinguish myself from my estimable older brother," he commented. "I'm pleased Lord Eamon invited me. It gives me the opportunity to expand my circle of acquaintances while doing an activity I greatly enjoy."

It appeared their host had gathered a group of men who would be a diverting party.

Rebecca and Lady Jocelyn made their entrance. The fetching pair received the guests with winning smiles and witty conversation. *Rebecca would have her pick of eligible bachelors here.* The disagreeable side of Kenneth wondered if her father had planned it so, but he knew that wasn't the case. Lord Eamon took his hunts very seriously.

"I hope to make your better acquaintance," Lady Jocelyn said to him.

"As do I," he replied, giving her his complete attention instead of watching Rebecca. "From what I understand, there'll be plenty of opportunities to rest and socialize apart from the contests."

He offered his arm, and they sat by the fireplace, talking about their travels. As a child, Lady Jocelyn spent time in France and Italy. She seemed a knowledgeable woman, and her command of languages sounded exceptional.

The younger participants joined them, Rebecca frowning as she took a seat.

Why would she frown at her friend? Or maybe she was frowning at me. That seems more likely, but I haven't done anything to her yet. Kenneth narrowed his eyes at her.

She made a face back.

The conversation turned towards his and Lord Spalding's sailing schemes, snatching Kenneth's preoccupation with Rebecca's facial expressions. Lord Spalding described what he hoped to ship.

"I told Mr. Barclay I wished to go with him on the maiden voyage," Rebecca said. "He flat out refused to take me."

I can't believe she spoke of that.

"Beautiful ladies asking to accompany me on long trips? I'd find a way to make that happen." Notley threw his arm along the back of his chair.

The men chuckled.

"I thought it made excellent sense for Mr. Barclay to decline," said Lady Jocelyn. "I can't imagine such a trip would be comfortable or safe."

Kenneth beamed at her. "Someone in the company is a sensible person."

"Apparently, Mr. Barclay has high standards, Miss Tarleton," said Mr. Fitzpatrick quietly. "You may have to sweeten the pot."

"I did. I made a deal impossible to pass over."

"Which was?" prompted Notley.

"If I lose the hunt, I'll invest in his next ship," Rebecca replied. "But if I win, he'd take me on the test trip."

Lord Spalding whistled. "Sounds like a great proposal. Why didn't you accept, Mr. Barclay?"

"I don't blame you for turning it down," Repington put in. "I wouldn't want to be shown up by Miss Tarleton either."

Notley and Mr. Fitzpatrick snickered.

Kenneth frowned. *What are these men all about?* "The deal didn't erase my initial objections. That voyage is not safe for a lady."

"Miss Tarleton can handle it," Repington said.

Rebecca gave Kenneth a smug expression.

He scowled. *Why are they ganging up on me? What men will do to curry a pretty woman's favor.*

"My daughter is stiff competition." Lord Eamon grinned like a Cheshire cat as he walked towards the group. "The equal of any man in skill and quite possibly better than Kenneth. She may be protecting him instead of the other way around."

"Oh," the other men hooted and hollered.

"I'm not afraid of Miss Tarleton," retorted Kenneth and then pointed at Rebecca. "I accept your deal. And further, the funds should be readily available because I'll start the next ship immediately after my voyage is over."

The company clapped and yelled their approval as Rebecca gave Kenneth a saucy expression. "You must win first, and I'll remind you I'm a champion."

The butler announced dinner was served, and the group headed towards the dining room.

Kenneth fell in step alongside Rebecca. "You always get your way, don't you?"

"Not always." She gloated. "Though beating you all the time does bring extra pleasure."

The two held the gaze a beat longer than necessary, and Kenneth cleared his throat as he looked away.

Now he had another challenge besides winning the tournament for investment money. He'd publicly vowed to build his next ship. He hadn't seriously considered, much less planned, his next project—until Rebecca goaded him into action.

*****

Rebecca

Rebecca took her place at the table. Showing Barclay up for his shooting skills might not be the way to win him, but she wouldn't slack because of it. *I'll compete that much harder.* She wasn't joking when she said she'd enjoy beating him.

"There are many kinds of competitions taking place here," Lady Jocelyn remarked to her. "It's interesting how Mr. Barclay seems to be in the center of them all."

I've unwittingly entered into one with her. Rebecca had a sense of it before, but Lady Jocelyn openly acknowledged it now.

I shouldn't fight guests over a gentleman, especially one I've invited for the purpose of... purpose of what? To play with a man's affections so she could gain back the attention of another? That was incredibly stupid and cruel of me. I could view this as a rescue mission. Save Barclay from Lady Jocelyn.

Lady Jocelyn raised an eyebrow and smiled at her. *I'm not backing down from anything.* Rebecca nodded. *Let the hunt begin.*

The Competition

Rebecca

The following morning, an elaborate breakfast had been cleared away, and the group gathered in the great room, eagerly awaiting the first day's challenge. Even though she wasn't participating, Lady Jocelyn was in a chair to Rebecca's right, and the Fitzpatrick brothers sat to her left.

Rebecca needed to be seen as a peer for the competition. She constantly assessed how to strike a balance between that and being considered a proper woman of her station. One slip up, and she could be done.

Along those lines, she paid careful attention to her wardrobe for the festivities and had several articles made especially for the events. The new archery jacket she currently wore was an attractive green color and cut that flattered her, but the sleeves were sewn to give her greater freedom of movement than her other jackets and dresses. She had special gloves that matched as well.

"Days one and two are archery events," Lord Eamon said as he stood in front of them. "Today we'll complete the stationary target contest, and tomorrow will be mounted archery."

Horseback archery was challenging, but she acquired skill during the last couple of years and enjoyed it immensely.

"I look forward to seeing your mounted archery skills, Miss Tarleton," said Lord Spalding.

"Will Miss Tarleton have an advantage to level the field?" asked Barclay, across from her.

Rebecca glared at him. *Barclay would be the one to thwart my goal of being a peer in this group. I need another romantic interest.*

Lord Putnam was seated next to him on the couch. "Why would we do that?"

"I'd like a chance at winning," quipped Repington. *At least they're in my corner.*

"Wouldn't mounted archery be too difficult for Miss Tarleton?" asked Kenneth.

I really, really need a new interest.

"I don't believe even all the men can do it well," Lady Jocelyn said to her. "Mr. Barclay's query seems an excellent one to ensure the event is fair and balanced."

Barclay smiled broadly at her.

"Which is why I hope Miss Tarleton gets absolutely no advantages," Repington said.

"Now I'm really excited to see this event." Lord Spalding rubbed his hands together.

"I've been doing it for years," Rebecca explained to Lady Jocelyn, trying not to sound annoyed or exasperated. "My father taught me, and we've received extensive training during our travels. I might not win, but I won't be an embarrassment either."

Lady Jocelyn raised an eyebrow. "You're quite confident then?"

"I have an accurate understanding of my skill level."

"There are no margins, leads, or any other manufactured advantages in this competition," her father announced. "I wouldn't have allowed Miss Tarleton to participate if I believed her incapable of holding her ground."

Barclay seemed doubtful but remained silent.

"Anyone who hits the bullseye receives a bonus for themselves and their team," Rebecca's father continued. "Four rounds, three arrows apiece. The competition begins in an hour. Any questions?"

After answering in the negative, everyone dispersed to prepare for day one.

*****

Kenneth

Kenneth surveyed his team as they gathered by the shooting line, the day overcast and the grass damp from the soaking the day before. He was pleased to be with Lord Spalding and Baxter, but he didn't know the other gentleman, Mr. Adams. A portly, jovial man with graying hair and dark eyes, he was another neighbor of Lord Eamon's. Mr. Adams had declared he needed an escape, and this gathering would be a welcome diversion from his family. Apparently, his son always asked for money, his eldest daughter constantly left her children with him and the missus, and his youngest daughter repeatedly spoke of her upcoming entrance into society the following season.

Kenneth was also happy he was teammates with Rebecca and would be close to her during the games. From what the others had commented, Kenneth surmised she must, at least, be able to hold her own. They were there for a friendly competition, but Kenneth aimed to win all the same.

However, he didn't want to seem like an ornery participant either. *I must relax and keep some of my comments to myself.* When he'd asked about Rebecca earlier, the company had regarded him with great amusement. He thought it a perfectly reasonable question, for he didn't know any women who could do mounted archery.

Rebecca had shot him a dagger look. *That isn't anything new. I can rely on her to maintain the status quo. The pig chase changed nothing about our acquaintance.*

Kenneth's disappointment perplexed him since he felt he couldn't court her. His declination seemed to only offend her dignity and nothing more. He had no desire to inflict pain by his decision, but at the same time, he wished she cared for him; that if he had pursued a relationship, she might have said yes.

That clearly wasn't going to happen.

"Lady Jocelyn seems quite the traveler," Kenneth commented to Rebecca, attempting normalcy, as they waited for the servants to finish setting up.

"I suppose," she replied. "She's no more well-traveled than I."

Kenneth reflected on that. As Rebecca had intimated earlier, she had accompanied her father on several trips. But Lady Jocelyn's travels were similar to the typical European tour, while the Tarletons had always gone to lands much further away. "She seems to have an impressive mastery of languages as a result."

"She does. Languages come easily to her. I suppose my command of Mongolian is wanting."

Kenneth shook his head, and they snapped to attention as Lord Eamon began the event. The teams drew a shooting order, and they would rotate each round to shoot with a different person.

Mr. Adams went first against Notley and scored a five.

Kenneth sighed. *This does not bode well.*

Fortunately for them, Notley didn't shoot much better, so the other team was only two points ahead at the end of the turn.

Baxter's performance against Repington was even worse, and they slid further behind. Lord Spalding did well, but his brother performed better and hit the first bullseye. Kenneth's team was now losing by twenty points.

He groaned when he realized he was competing against his father. Lord Putnam was more skilled, and he scrambled Kenneth's thinking faculties.

"It's nothing more than a friendly competition," Father called and then snickered.

Does he thrive on beating up on me? Kenneth's performance was mediocre, while his father hit a bullseye.

Their team was losing badly.

Rebecca stepped up to the line against her father. She pulled back on the bow, and her muscles slackened.

She hit a six.

That was what Kenneth first scored, so he couldn't be critical.

Rebecca bit her lip as her body relaxed into the second shot like she was attempting to become one with the arrow and struck a nine.

Kenneth glanced at her sharply.

Acting unaware of everyone around her, Rebecca pulled the last arrow from her quiver, maintaining eye contact towards the target the whole time.

I've never seen this level of concentration from her before.

Rebecca's last shot was an eight. Lord Eamon edged her out by only a few points.

Kenneth stared at her. *She beat me.*

After round one, Rebecca was second on their team and fifth overall — in the center of the pack.

Mr. Adams congratulated her.

"Thank you," she replied. "But I'll have to perform better next round."

And perform better she did.

Rebecca shot nothing but nines and bullseyes after round one. It was hard for Kenneth to keep from gawking at her. While his performance was decent, Rebecca ranked first on their team and fourth in the tournament standings by the end of the event.

Kenneth didn't like losing to her, but the fact she beat him with such a composed countenance and demeanor increased her appeal. Greatly. Gone was the giddy-headed girl he'd known. This was a woman who could handle herself.

And he liked it.

"Miss Tarleton, the rumors are true," Lord Spalding said. "Very well done."

"You're the only reason we haven't been completely squashed," Mr. Adams said to her. "Your father, Lord Putnam, and Mr. Fitzpatrick are beastly."

"They must have their weak areas," Notley remarked. "We'll see how it all pans out. I don't think we made a bad showing."

Kenneth could hold his own with archery, but the mounted variety was not his strong suit.

What other surprises will Rebecca unleash?

CHAPTER 10

Dead Last

Rebecca

The first day was even more enjoyable than Rebecca had imagined it would be. Papa's highly amusing guests made the evening lively, and Rebecca's team welcomed her as one of them.

The following day, the group was on the lawn behind the house for the mounted archery contest. The sun gifted them with an appearance, and the skies were clear. Rebecca knew it would be challenging to beat her father and Lord Putnam, but Mr. Fitzpatrick was a surprise, and she was eager to see his skills in the other games.

"How many outfits do you have on?" Barclay asked.

"Only you would note that," Rebecca retorted. "I'm sure every other man here doesn't care a whit."

Rebecca wore a longer, deep blue jacket. She refused to ride side-saddle for these contests but couldn't be utterly scandalous, so she had a dress and special pants designed for this event. Though peculiar, the outfit should allow her to ride effectively, maintain decency, of sorts, and be warm.

"Rebecca, you're first," her father said. "Why don't you show the fellows how we ride?" He winked at her.

She grinned. "Gladly."

The first course was straight with five targets and would test their speed. The fastest and most accurate performance won.

Rebecca climbed on Mason with her bow and quiver. Her father had been working with her so she could hold more than one arrow at a time. She could do two, but three would be risky, though advantageous in this setup.

She and Mason started down the grassy path. Rebecca stuck with two arrows and increased her speed.

One. That shot felt good.

Two. The release wasn't as clean, but still not bad.

She snatched her next two arrows as she zeroed in on the next target fast approaching.

Three. Blast. That wasn't a clean shot.

Four. Redeemed herself.

Rebecca whipped out the last arrow quick and sharp and shot.

Bullseye.

Lord Spalding whistled and clapped as she rode Mason back to the gentlemen. "Miss Tarleton, I may need to seek your hand in marriage."

Rebecca chuckled. "Be careful, Lord Spalding. I might say yes."

He laughed.

Barclay wore an odd expression. "Where'd you learn to shoot like that?"

"Papa has repeatedly told you I know what I'm doing, and you refuse to believe him."

"There's knowing what you're doing, and then there's your performance. That was spectacular."

Rebecca glowed. "Thank you."

"You're our sole hope here, Gregory," said Lord Putnam. "Unless Mr. Fitzpatrick is as able on horseback as he is on foot."

Mr. Fitzpatrick shook his head. "I'll stay upright and hit the target, but don't expect a high point total."

Lady Jocelyn walked over. "Miss Tarleton, you looked romantically unbridled out there. No wonder Mr. Barclay called you a wild woman."

Rebecca fought a frown. Lady Jocelyn didn't say that in a way that sounded complimentary, and there was nothing uncontrolled about this event. She had to maintain the deepest concentration to accomplish it.

Be polite. Lady Jocelyn is my friend, though I'm unsure what kind of sordid friendship this is morphing into. "Thank you, Lady Jocelyn."

Everyone's performance slid, and true to Lord Putnam's prediction, Papa kept his team ahead, though the gap narrowed.

The second course wouldn't have a time component, but the circuit was round to add an extra challenge to accuracy.

Repington shook his head. "Do you wish me dead, Lord Eamon?"

"Just keeping things interesting," he responded.

"I suppose you practice this as well?" Barclay asked Rebecca.

"Of course," she replied.

"Why don't you do these activities when you visit instead of the silly nonsense?"

Rebecca narrowed her eyes. "Maybe the silly nonsense is what you choose to see."

"Are you truly asserting you're a serious person?"

"I have a sense of humor. Try it."

"We adults need to engage in dignified behavior."

"You fuss more than Mr. Baxter's baby girl," Rebecca snapped. "Instead of complaining, why don't you do something?"

"Like building ships and making trade agreements? But you wouldn't know about those matters. The only trades you make are money for dresses."

"What's your obsession with my clothing? Have your eyes gotten their fill?"

Barclay clenched his jaw. "Why look at you when a far more polite lady is in our presence?"

"You would like anyone who quotes you." Rebecca stepped into his space. "Makes you feel important and not like your father's whipping boy—"

Lord Spalding cleared his throat. "As entertaining as this is, I think we should bring the intensity down a bit."

Rebecca stepped back.

"Are you in a good enough frame of mind to begin, Rebecca?" her father asked quietly.

She snatched her bow. "I always perform when needed." She marched over to Mason and shot a near-perfect score on the second course.

Rebecca rode by Barclay when she was done. "Do something about that."

The other men chuckled — except Barclay. His eyes flashed.

I'm definitely dead last in Barclay's affections. Maybe I'm better off there.

CHAPTER 11

Affinity

Kenneth

Rebecca had the nerve to perform flawlessly, as though their argument didn't bother her. She rose through the rankings while Kenneth dropped to the bottom five as he turned himself inside out over their spat. *Why does she do this to me?*

The other men didn't understand why Kenneth was so contentious with Rebecca. He had no suitable answer for them other than the truth, which he didn't wish to divulge.

I have to regain control of myself. He'd acted like a lunatic, even though the others found the spectacle comical and seemed to take everything in stride. Besides Rebecca, his father appeared the most upset and glared at him for the rest of the afternoon. Lord Eamon was cool towards Kenneth, but that was understandable.

Rebecca was second on the leader board for the competition by the challenge's end.

Kenneth and Notley took a ride through the woods afterward.

"You and Miss Tarleton seem extremely well acquainted." Notley grinned.

"We've known each other for an eternity, and it feels like it," Kenneth grumbled.

"I think your exasperation is exaggerated."

Kenneth tried to hide his embarrassment. He knew the other men appreciated her beauty and manner. *Lady Jocelyn was the one I wanted to get to know better. Why can't I maintain focus on that?*

"It seems as though there's strong affinity," Notley commented.

"An affinity for driving each other insane."

"That sounds like a marvelous courtship to me. I can only dream of meeting a girl that drove me that wild."

"I appreciate being in my right mind, thank you, and would rather court a woman that kept me there." *Rebecca wouldn't have me anyway.*

"You shouldn't dismiss Miss Tarleton. She's an extraordinary person."

"Do I come off dismissive?"

Notley shot him a look.

"I don't mean to be." *Of course, she doesn't want to court me. Why would she court someone who disparages her? I treat Rebecca as a little girl, but she's a grown woman. Why is it so hard to adjust my view?*

*****

Rebecca

The idea of knocking things into one another appealed to Rebecca after the mounted archery competition, so she set up a bocce game for herself, though it was rather cool outside for this kind of activity.

The ignoramus.

She threw her first ball, which slammed into the

target ball.

Why do I care for someone who doesn't think much for me? Rebecca pitched another ball. This one didn't come close. *I deserve better than this.* She tossed a third.

"Would you like a partner?" a man asked.

Rebecca looked up, and Lord Putnam gave her a rare, warm smile as he walked her way.

"Certainly," she replied. "It'd be more enjoyable."

Unlike his son at present, Lord Putnam treated her with appreciation, and Rebecca enjoyed her time with him. He possessed a reputation for being high-handed and a little rough, especially in business matters, but Rebecca had never seen that side of him.

They restarted the game, and he inquired after her current pursuits and how her investments were doing. They lapsed into companionable silence as they played for a while.

"Please, be patient with my son," Lord Putnam said. "If he weren't so caught in the past, he'd have asked you to court already."

Rebecca's cheeks heated. She'd always kept this little secret very close to her heart. *He must have detected something to say such a thing. I rather not reveal a fondness for his son before there's any understanding. How mortifying.* "You heard the awful row we had in public. He'll never ask to court me." She threw a ball. "And he treats me like a child."

"I know. If it'll ease your consternation, Kenneth doesn't see many matters clearly at the outset. I love my son, but there are days..." He exhaled as he tossed the ball. "I understand your frustration."

Despite herself, Rebecca grinned.

"That row is the reason I'm asking, because it's evidence he's strongly attracted to you and doesn't want to admit it," Lord Putnam explained.

Rebecca bit her lip. She figured that was the case,

but Barclay's behavior caused her to second guess herself. And in the end, Barclay may decide, as he'd told her, not to pursue anything, no matter his true affections.

This was a bizarre conversation with Lord Putnam, but oddly, it eased her mind to discuss the matter in more detail than she had with her father.

"Kenneth's heart is usually in the right place," Lord Putnam said. "But he's naïve and sensitive. Arrogant and tentative."

Rebecca was amused. "Do you want me to like Barclay?"

Lord Putnam laughed. "You're sensible enough to perceive what's behind the fog. I'm asking you to please allow more time for it to clear. He'll get there."

"I'm surprised you'd choose me for your son and heir."

"You're perfect for him. Most people pat him on the back and tell him he's fine, and objectively, yes, he could do far worse."

Rebecca chuckled.

"He has it in him to accomplish incredible things if he knuckled down and made some adjustments. But anytime I say something — he and I are oil and water, as you well know. I make him more determined to hold to his ways, and we drive one another up the tall timbers. My largest motivation for giving him Laidley Park, at this time, was to separate us so he could pursue his talents and interests free of my interference."

"My father and I had wondered."

"You force Kenneth to see the negative too, but he'll attempt to alter it instead of holding fast. He can be himself and still change. There are precious few people with that power over him, and he'll be a better person for it."

"I believe you overrate me, sir."

"I think not. We're fortunate you're giving us any consideration."

I was about to give up Barclay for good, but I won't yet.

CHAPTER 12

Create Yourself

Kenneth

Wednesday morning, Kenneth's team gawked at one another as the new rules were announced. Today and tomorrow's challenge was to hunt for their dinners and prepare them for everyone. They could choose to use the kitchen or go very basic and cook on an open fire outside. Mr. Adams offered to stay behind to do the preparation, and Spalding quickly claimed Baxter as a partner, leaving Kenneth with Rebecca.

This day will be eternal.

Rebecca's appearance reminded Kenneth of an attractive version of the woods they were in. Her long, well-fitting duster-like jacket complimented an evergreen dress, and she wore a sensible cap and boots.

At first, they were quiet, concentrating on the task at hand. They never spoke to one another after their argument, so there was that distance as well.

After Kenneth's indignation had dissipated, he felt guilty for his cutting words. Rebecca may exasperate and even anger him occasionally, but she didn't deserve to be treated in the way he had dealt with her. If anyone had spoken to his sisters in such a manner, he would've been all over them. It was a wonder her father hadn't berated him as he'd been quite benign when Kenneth had met with him last night.

"I apologize for my sharp comments yesterday," he said after they'd been together for some time. "Our familiarity isn't an excuse for rudeness when I'm with you."

"I'm sorry as well and can stand to remember the same thing." Rebecca bit her lip. "My words were harsh. I shouldn't have said them, especially in company."

"They were true." *She has a knack for pinpointing truths regarding my person with embarrassing clarity. I need to be a stronger gentleman and take it.* "My statements weren't accurate, only a lashing out to hurt back."

Rebecca grimaced. "You succeeded."

Kenneth's heart struck him. "That's not success. I must do better, and I'll endeavor to behave as a gentleman ought towards you." He held a hand out. "Truce?"

"Truce." Rebecca shook it and then inquired after his two younger sisters.

"They're to see Lady Corwyn shortly."

"Your break with her didn't affect their friendship?" she asked tentatively.

He shook his head. "I'm glad for it, as odd as that might sound. The girls were as close as sisters, and it's not as though Hannah seriously wronged me."

"It's still good of you to have those sentiments. Rational thought doesn't always go hand in hand with our feelings."

Kenneth gave a rough laugh. "True indeed."

"It's wonderful they could form that kind of relationship with one another."

"You sound as though you envy it."

She nodded. "I've never had a friend that close to me."

"I thought you were quite popular amongst your set."

"There's a difference between popularity and genuine friendship. Other than my father, I've not formed a strong attachment to anyone, though I felt your sister and Hannah would be excellent choices for companionship."

"At least you have your father. I never felt close to mine."

"You two seem very different," Rebecca remarked. "Do you take after your mother then?"

"Perhaps. As my sister grows older, she's quite like Mama."

"Do you miss your mama terribly?" Rebecca asked.

"I do. We were a more cohesive family when she was alive, even with a good stepmother. Do you miss not having a mother?"

"I loved being raised by Father, and it's not like he's uninvolved. But I've observed many mothers guide and oversee their daughters' courtships. Sometimes, I wish for that."

"Especially with blockheads like me, right?"

Rebecca stared towards the ground. "You are perplexing, Barclay."

"That's generous of you to say." He cleared his throat. "Do you think you'd be much different if your mother had survived?"

"I'm sure her presence in my life would've had some effect. I'd possibly be more ladylike. Your shots about me being a wild woman hit home."

He winced. "I shouldn't have said those things. It's as though I get around you and forget myself," he trailed off, coming dangerously close to admitting things he did not want.

"You spoke your true thoughts," Rebecca said. "I can believe you think me without every rule of propriety, and there are days when I think that of myself."

"You're refined, and your other skills and qualities make you more unique."

Rebecca gave him a dubious look.

"In a positive way," he clarified.

"There are times I rather be ordinary and blend in."

"Believe me, it's overrated," he muttered.

"You think you're like everyone else?"

Kenneth shrugged. "I have nothing to distinguish myself with. I'm Lord Putnam's son. And while there are far worse things to be, it's like I don't possess my own identity." He considered her for a moment. "You're very much your own person and known as such. I envy and admire you for that."

The air grew heavy, like the instant in the barn. Kenneth snatched himself from her hold on him.

"You have Laidley Park as well as this ship and trade project with Lord Spalding," Rebecca said. "Perhaps now is your time to create yourself."

"I hope so," Kenneth said.

As he cleaned up for their early afternoon break between sessions, he reflected on their conversation. *I've never been so honest with someone.*

And it's fitting it was with Rebecca.

CHAPTER 13

The Visitor

Kenneth

"I'd like to accompany you this afternoon, if I may," Lady Jocelyn asked after the company had taken a break for a light midday eat.

"I'm sure that can be arranged," replied Kenneth. The men exchanged glances with one another.

Rebecca shot Kenneth a look and then smoothed her face as she turned towards Lady Jocelyn. "You can come with Mr. Barclay and me if you wish."

"Perfect. What would be appropriate attire?"

Rebecca rattled off brief instructions, and Lady Jocelyn left the room.

"Why did you agree to her request so quickly?" Rebecca asked him in a harsh whisper.

"I understand wishing to go, but I didn't think it through."

Rebecca sighed. "I can keep her entertained, but then you'll have to do most of the legwork this afternoon."

The morning had been productive for their team, but they required more.

The butler entered the great room. "Mr. Adams, your son is here and requires a moment of your time."

His face grew stormy.

"Perhaps it's an emergency," Lord Eamon said.

"An emergency because he stiffed the man who spotted him money for his gambling debts, and now the lender wants blood." Mr. Adams growled. "I'll see to him and then return." He strode out of the room.

The rest of the group dispersed, leaving Kenneth and Rebecca waiting for Lady Jocelyn.

"What is delaying her?" Rebecca exclaimed.

"Patience. Try not to hurt your friend."

Rebecca scowled at him instead.

Lady Jocelyn finally appeared in raiment, not entirely appropriate for hunting but pleasing all the same.

"Usually, we ride a little way into the woods, tie up the horses, and then go on foot. Will that suit you?" Kenneth offered his arm to Lady Jocelyn as they walked outside.

"What other solution is there?" Rebecca asked. "We can't hunt game on the house grounds."

Kenneth threw her a look. *Would you simmer down?*

"That should be fine, as long as we don't walk too far." Lady Jocelyn replied. "The woods sound like a dangerous place." She grinned as though she believed the opposite.

Rebecca's features suddenly appeared strained, as though she were attempting to gain control of her breathing.

Kenneth wanted to help but was unsure how. *It's a wonder she still goes into the woods as often as she does. Fighting with and through things like a conqueror. I'll give her a minute.*

Kenneth turned towards Lady Jocelyn. "Danger is seldom encountered there, but be alert and respectful, and we should be quite safe."

Lady Jocelyn stopped walking. "Perhaps we shouldn't do this then."

"You asked to come," Rebecca said tightly. "We'll be fine. I'm winning this challenge."

A slow smirk slid across Lady Jocelyn's face, and Rebecca stormed into the stables, leaving Kenneth staring after her.

"She seems in a mood today," Lady Jocelyn said. "It's a wonder you could spend the entire morning with her."

"It was a pleasant one," Kenneth replied.

Annoyance flitted over Lady Jocelyn's features before she flashed him a brilliant smile. "I'm happy to hear that."

"Rebecca was lost and injured in the woods as a young girl and nearly died. She's allowed some defensiveness."

"Of course, I didn't know."

"The afternoon is wasting," Rebecca called. "I'll wait for the two of you on the path." She rode past them.

Lady Jocelyn watched her. "Quite the little commander with this, isn't she?"

Kenneth shrugged. "She is, but she's correct. We need to move along."

He helped Lady Jocelyn onto a horse, and the trio set out.

Kenneth and Rebecca were decent riders, so they could make short work of a trip into the forest when it was the two of them. Lady Jocelyn wasn't as experienced, so they didn't travel deep into the woods.

"Mr. Barclay, could I bother you for your arm again?" Lady Jocelyn asked after they'd dismounted.

He was already holding a rifle and had a small bag around him.

Rebecca made a soft growling sound and held out her hand.

Kenneth passed her his rifle and then smiled at Lady Jocelyn as he lent her his arm. "Of course."

"This terrain is tougher than I thought it would be," Lady Jocelyn remarked as she took it. "There wasn't something less wilderness-like?"

"We're headed into the forest to hunt game for food," Rebecca answered. "What did you think it'd be like?"

Lady Jocelyn narrowed her eyes. "Why are you so cross with me?" She pouted at Kenneth. "Have I been so disagreeable that my friend would treat me thus?"

"No, of course not." Kenneth gave Rebecca another look.

Rebecca appeared as though she were about to boil over and strode away from them.

Lady Jocelyn asked him a few questions about Laidley Park and Putnam.

"You two must stop talking. I'm going eastward a bit." Rebecca moved away from them.

"We'll catch nothing if we don't quiet down," Kenneth explained to Lady Jocelyn. "Rebecca, I require my gun," he called after her.

She returned and smirked. "Will you be able to use it?" she asked quietly.

Kenneth tried to appear disapproving but ended up fighting the urge to laugh instead.

Rebecca flashed him a wry grin as she handed it over.

"Perhaps we can find a log or rock for you to sit upon," he said to Lady Jocelyn.

Her eyes widened. "You won't leave me?"

Rebecca was right; this is turning into a hassle. "No, I'll stay within eyeshot of you." He directed his attention to Rebecca. "I understand wanting some distance between us, but you shouldn't wander far either. There's a reason we're in pairs."

"I'll periodically give a low whistle like this—" Rebecca demonstrated.

"Very good," Kenneth replied, and she took off.

"She really is a wild woman," Lady Jocelyn remarked.

"After her experience in the woods, she and her father made sure she was equipped to handle anything."

"I'd think it'd be easier to forbid her from going."

"You don't know the Tarletons very well. We must cease talking if I'm to get anything done."

Lady Jocelyn nodded, and they fell into silence.

Kenneth walked away from her, scanning his surroundings. These woods were a little different from the forests of Putnam, but he still felt like he was at home, maybe even more so here.

After a while, Kenneth heard rustling in some brush. He carefully crouched down to blend in better. A twig snapped, and a lady screamed.

Kenneth sprung up and whipped his head towards Lady Jocelyn. He could hardly make her out, so he ran towards her. "What's wrong?" he asked breathlessly.

"I heard a snap and thought I was to be pounced upon!" she cried, her eyes huge and face pale.

Kenneth sighed.

Rebecca raced towards them. "What's the matter?"

Kenneth shook his head. "Nothing. We're fine."

"We might as well go in for the day," Rebecca said. "There won't be a thing around now, and it'll be too late by the time we get a new spot."

"Were you able to catch anything?" Kenneth asked.

"Quail," Rebecca replied. "Hopefully, we can retrieve it on our return."

"How will you get it back?" Lady Jocelyn asked, eyes wide.

"I'll bag it, and it'll stay with me," Kenneth replied

"You're traveling with a dead animal?" Lady Jocelyn's voice was high. "Can't the servants get it?"

"They have for a couple of the other pairs, and they might have to for us if we can't find it," Kenneth answered. "But it's simply a bird; we can take care of it."

Lady Jocelyn scrunched her face.

Rebecca sighed. "Let's go in."

Kenneth stared at Rebecca's retreating back as Lady Jocelyn took his arm once more. *I made a mess of things. Again.*

CHAPTER 14

Partners

Rebecca

On Thursday, Father assigned partners for the second day of the supper hunting event, and Rebecca was paired with Barclay. She was annoyed with him for yesterday, though she supposed most of it wasn't his fault. More than likely, it was disappointment that their time together had been ruined after a surprisingly marvelous morning. She'd never had such a sincere conversation with Barclay.

The two set off, quiet in the beginning like the day before.

"I'm sorry about yesterday afternoon," Barclay said after a while.

Rebecca's annoyance evaporated with his apology. "It's not your fault. You were polite. Something I could have made a better attempt towards."

"Have you and Lady Jocelyn been friends for long?"

"No, I met her in London this past spring," she replied. "What kept you away this year?"

"I was there for a couple of weeks but not inclined to remain long as my attention was divided."

"Lady Jocelyn divided your attention," Rebecca remarked quietly. "Do you think you might pay her more?"

"Lady Jocelyn holds one in a spell for a while, and once it breaks, leaves them yearning for something of substance."

"You wish for a wife with that quality?" Rebecca asked carefully.

Barclay glanced at her, and she looked away.

"Of course," he replied.

Rebecca's chest twisted. *And he chose not to court me because he doesn't see me as someone of substance.* "What else?"

"I don't know as well as I should." He gave her a wry smile. "If you'll recall, I barely have an identity. It's difficult to imagine a wife I'd be happy with."

Rebecca stared at him.

"Yes?" he asked.

"That carried more depth than I ever gave you credit for."

Barclay chuckled. "And here I thought I was the one being dismissive."

"I don't mean to minimize you, Barclay. My feelings are quite the reverse."

The two lapsed into silence for a time so they could accomplish the tasks at hand.

"What induces you to choose the men you court?" he asked her.

Rebecca stilled. "That's a highly personal question."

"You inquired if I was interested in Lady Jocelyn. That was personal."

True. Rebecca couldn't expound on how she chose her suitors because the reasons involved Barclay. "I favor gentlemen I hope will occupy my attention and distract me from other things." *Like not being with Barclay.*

"So you're not seriously considering a marriage partner?"

"I am, but my foremost choice isn't seriously considering me." This conversation unsettled her. "Why the interest in my interests?"

"Every man I speak with who's acquainted with you shouts your praises, and many of them are of high caliber. I'm surprised you haven't chosen one of them."

"Matters of the heart aren't always that simple."

The two fell into silence again, the air taking on that heavy quality that descended upon them when they were together, even though it was a brisk November day.

Barclay cleared his throat. "If you're agreeable, Lord Spalding suggested I partner with you again for Monday's challenge, and he'd work with Mr. Baxter."

The event would be a long course with mystery targets spread throughout the grounds of the estate and the forest's edge. Father had described the challenge and furnished maps for the route earlier that morning. The event would test their speed and accuracy as well as their observation and endurance. Various sections of the course had differing point values, and partners could switch off. Lord Eamon wouldn't participate in this event, and Mr. Adams had offered to sit out to make the pairings equal.

Strategically, Lord Spalding's suggestion made perfect sense. He and Rebecca were the team's top scorers, so separating them was a good idea. However, the way Barclay had asked lit a tiny flame of hope inside her that he might see her in another light and make a different choice. "That's a fine idea," she replied.

"I suggest we strategize prior to the event."

Rebecca agreed a battle plan would be wise. "Did you want to discuss it on our way back?"

"I'd prefer to meet up later, perhaps before dinner after we've cleaned up and rested a bit."

Her breathing picked up a little. "I'll be in the library around three."

"Perfect."

They finished their present challenge in silence.

*****

Kenneth

Kenneth watched Rebecca climb the stairs after they returned.

His father had said she'd be excellent for him. *I dismissed that because I underestimated her, and I shouldn't have.*

Kenneth grew restless, like he was on the verge of losing something valuable.

I need to court her.

The clarity of that thought left him with an urgency that startled him, as though being shocked to life. *I'll ride and figure out how to fix things since I've been such a numbskull towards her lately.*

He was on his way out the door when Lady Jocelyn intercepted him. "Mr. Barclay, precisely the gentleman I hoped to run into."

"How may I be of service?"

"Would you take a turn with me in the gardens? It's been rather lonely here this morning while everyone was away."

Kenneth hesitated. He had enough time to ride and then clean up for his meet with Rebecca, but probably not for all three tasks. *Perhaps the walk will be sufficient to help clear my mind.* "I'd be happy to accompany you, though I'm not in the best of dress."

"I like the rough and rugged apparel," she replied. "It suits you."

Kenneth raised an eyebrow. *No one has called me rough and rugged in my life.* "Then let's be off."

After Lady Jocelyn collected her hat and jacket, the two were in the gardens. Stoddard Grove had little in the way of flowers, especially this time of year, but a nice collection of trees, hedges, and a colossal fountain made the walk pleasant.

"I wish Miss Tarleton would take off one day and keep me company," Lady Jocelyn remarked. "I had no idea when I accepted the invitation that I'd be left to my own devices so much."

"You weren't aware Miss Tarleton was to participate?"

"No, she informed me when she issued the invite," Lady Jocelyn replied. "I imagined that as her guest, she'd adjust her participation. Most other ladies would." She chuckled. "But then most other ladies wouldn't take part in this sort of activity."

Kenneth set his jaw. "There may be something you could do to assist with the festivities."

Lady Jocelyn studied him. "You're quite taken with Miss Tarleton, aren't you?"

"I've known her since we were children. I speak to and of her more carelessly than I should, and I'm working to correct myself on that score. It annoys me to hear others talk of her in the same manner."

"You thought my comments vicious?"

"I thought them needlessly negative, which is curious coming from a friend of hers."

"I wouldn't blame you for being drawn to Miss Tarleton." She brushed her hand over the top of a hedge. "Many young men are. She had her choice of gentlemen to court when we were in London together, but I sensed she never cared much for them." She smiled coyly at him. "Perhaps because she preferred another not in our company at the time?"

Kenneth sighed. He hated when women spoke in riddles. *Why can't they simply state their meaning?* "What are you angling at, Lady Jocelyn?"

She burst into laughter. "You really have no clue, do you?"

He drew his brows together. "No clue about what?"

"I believe Miss Tarleton is half in love with you."

Kenneth stopped dead in his tracks. "You must be mistaken."

"I'm in earnest and most likely correct."

"Surely, she does not regard me in such a manner." His steps were more agitated as he began walking again, almost tripping on the stone path. *That's impossible.*

Wonderfully impossible.

Rebecca didn't shove me away when I kissed her. She punched the last gentleman who tried that on her, so it's not wholly inconceivable.

But if she's been interested in me all this time... He made a mental review of their interactions from the perspective of her liking him and winced.

"Of course, as taken with her as you might be, I'm sure you wouldn't think seriously upon her. I'd imagine you'd rather be with someone more refined and ladylike."

Kenneth scowled. He had to admit those were his thoughts in the past, but it angered him to hear Lady Jocelyn speak poorly of Rebecca in that backhanded manner. *Ladylike. What does that even mean? Rebecca is a phenomenal woman.*

"Come now, I didn't mean to pick a fight," said Lady Jocelyn. "Tell me more about this ship you're building for Lord Spalding. It sounds fascinating."

Kenneth talked about the project, and soon they were discussing their families. They crossed paths with Baxter and Mr. Adams, who said they were heading in to prepare for dinner.

"Is it that late already?" Kenneth asked in alarm.

"Yes, dinner will be in an hour," Baxter replied.

Kenneth excused himself in a hurry, asking if the men would escort Lady Jocelyn back to the house as he had forgotten about an important appointment.

CHAPTER 15

Catapult

Rebecca

I should have known.

Rebecca stomped out of the library towards the stables. *Why do I persist in torturing myself by hoping things will change?* She plopped the saddle on Mason, and he neighed.

"You're quite right. I'm taking this out on you."

The hurt was more piercing than ever, and Rebecca took a deep breath as it became harder to breathe. Earlier, she'd heard Lady Jocelyn ask Barclay to walk with her. Rebecca had hoped he'd be back for their meet. She squeezed her eyes tight as they grew hot. Anger was normal, but this reaction was new.

Something nudged her head, and she opened her eyes.

Mason stood before her.

She draped her arms around his neck and leaned against him. A few minutes later, Rebecca drove Mason out of the stables at a gallop. She continued at that pace for a while, slowly calming down. Dinner would be served soon, and she needed to dress and be a proper hostess.

She was walking her horse towards his bay when Barclay called behind her.

Rebecca's peaceful state vanished as a jolt of anger shot through her. She handed the reins to the stable master and asked him to tend to Mason.

"Rebecca." Barclay caught up to her. "I apologize—"

Rebecca whirled on him. "I consider myself a patient person, but I've had it with the condescending manner in which you treat me."

She strode towards the house.

"You're absolutely right, Miss Tarleton, and I beg your pardon," Barclay called after her.

Rebecca wavered. *That sounded like genuine remorse in his voice.* "Did you enjoy your walk with Lady Jocelyn?" she asked evenly.

"Not really, though I've had to endure worse, so I won't speak badly of her. If it helps, we spent a good deal of time discussing you."

"And how much of it was complimentary?"

"I deserve that, given our history."

"I'm sure Lady Jocelyn does as well."

"And yet, realizing that, I don't understand why you chose her as a close companion."

"I'm wondering myself." She paused. "The same could be said of you."

"You consider me a close companion?" he asked quietly.

Rebecca opened her mouth and then snapped it shut, not knowing how she should answer. "We've always been familiar, sometimes overly so, and I seem to be speaking to you as such during this hunt, so I suppose you've become one."

"How do you feel about that development?"

What an odd question. "I'd be happier if it were more reciprocal."

"I've shared things with you I haven't with anyone else."

"It's nice to know I'm not the only one spilling their deep, dark secrets," she said wryly.

Barclay chuckled. "No, indeed."

Rebecca's heart flip-flopped. *I love it when he's laughing with me and not at me, like the day we chased pigs. That was the perfect afternoon.*

"If I didn't permanently mess up my chances with you, may we meet tomorrow after dinner?" Barclay asked.

Rebecca swallowed. *I don't want to get my hopes up again.* "That would be fine."

"Excellent. Thank you for your forbearance and graciousness. Have a wonderful evening, Miss Tarleton." Barclay bowed and then walked away.

Rebecca gazed after him.

*****

Kenneth

The next day, early Friday afternoon, the group surrounded Lord Eamon's catapult contraption in a field a short ride from the house. The event had been postponed for a couple of hours until the rain finished and things dried out a bit.

"You like it?" boomed Lord Eamon.

Kenneth's father seemed amused. "How long did it take to construct this?"

"Been at it all spring and summer with carpenters and mechanical workers," Lord Eamon replied proudly. "Rebecca helped too."

"I wasn't a willing accomplice."

"Can I test it out?" asked Lord Spalding.

"Certainly!" exclaimed Lord Eamon.

A servant wheeled over a large basket with burlap bags, splattering mud along the way.

Repington inquired about the contents in the bags as Lord Spalding loaded one onto the catapult.

"Who's shooting?" Spalding asked. "We can't allow this to go to waste."

Kenneth's father raised his rifle. "I'm ready."

Lord Spalding released the safety on the catapult and pulled back on the arm. He let go, and the arm whipped up, propelling the sack high and far into the air. "Whoa!" he walloped.

Kenneth's father shot, and a white powdery material fell through the air. He lowered his rifle. "That's impressive, Gregory. What was in that bag?"

"Flour, I believe," he replied. "Since the bags have various substances, they should fly differently."

Mr. Fitzpatrick clapped his hands. "Let's begin. I'm ready to take a shot."

"Papa!" a high-pitched voice called behind them.

The group turned, and a girl who appeared to be about sixteen was crossing the grounds with the house-keeper.

"What's she doing here?" Mr. Adams asked.

The company stared at him.

"My daughter," he clarified. "But I don't under-stand why she's here."

The adolescent and an apologetic housekeeper approached them. "Lord Eamon, Miss Ada said she was looking for her father."

"Miss Ada, how are you this morning?" Lord Ea-mon asked.

"Much better now, thank you." She beamed as she surveyed the group.

"Why are you here?" Mr. Adams asked her, baffled.

"Nothing was exciting enough to hold me at home, so I decided to visit you. And I'm very glad I did." Her cheeks grew pink as she giggled.

Mr. Adams sighed. "Lord Eamon, do you have any qualms with my daughter accompanying us a bit today? I know it's not what you've envisioned."

"It's fine," he answered. "Miss Ada might enjoy the catapult."

"Catapult!" she exclaimed as Lord Spalding loaded the next bag. "Sounds positively medieval. How delightful."

Kenneth stood by Rebecca. He was having difficulty bridging the gap between whatever they currently were to something more, especially since he'd squandered the perfect occasion before. For now, he stayed near Rebecca, hoping that would increase his chances and opportunities.

"I wonder at Miss Ada's enthusiasm for being here," he commented to Rebecca.

She gave a soft laugh. "I don't."

Barclay raised an eyebrow at her.

"A sixteen-year-old girl suddenly surrounded by a group of young, attractive, rich gentlemen. She was very honest when she said she was delighted to be here."

I completely missed that angle. "You're into making catapults?"

"Yes, the wild woman I am," she replied wryly.

"I wouldn't call this wild," Kenneth said. "More like a novel. It takes skill to get a catapult working as well as you two did."

"Thank you, but that was mostly Papa. I merely tweaked a couple of things so the bags would fly farther out instead of high in the air."

"Impressive still."

"It's not what I want to be known for in company."

Kenneth studied her. "I'm surprised you care so much."

"That doesn't shock me."

He winced. "No, I meant I think of you as mastering and conquering everything in sight. You're destroying this competition."

Rebecca grinned.

"Couldn't you do something similar when you're out?" Kenneth asked.

Her smile faltered. "It's not that simple. This makes sense. The laws of physics and of nature — I can handle those. The peculiarities of people?" She shook her head. "Those are mysterious."

"You must have some understanding of people. You're well-liked."

"Am I?" She gazed at him a moment. "And even if that were so, it can be fleeting."

Kenneth took a step towards her. "Rebecca," he began in a lowered tone. "There's nothing—"

"Rebecca!" her father called. "I want you to try it out now."

She walked off to take her turn.

Is she unsure of herself? I can scarcely believe that. Kenneth had met few people who were more confident than Rebecca. She always blasted her way through everything. That same quality had led him to believe she was immature.

His heart sank. *What if I contributed to Rebecca's uncertainty by undermining her? It's not as though I've been cheering for her lately. I never imagined I held that kind of power.*

I must change.

CHAPTER 16

Miss Tarleton

Kenneth

"His Grace, The Duke of Hartwell, has arrived," the butler announced during dinner the following evening.

Lord Eamon wiped his mouth and threw his napkin on the table. "Excellent! He's expected. Show him in."

This was a rather informal gathering for Lord Eamon to entertain a duke. It would appear the viscount moved in higher circles than Kenneth had ever realized. Lord Spalding would inherit a marquisette one day, and it was plain he and Lord Eamon were close.

The women exchanged glances, and then Lady Jocelyn eyed him as though she were the cat and he the canary.

Why is she smiling at me in that manner?

A tall, good-looking man about Kenneth's age with dark hair and eyes walked into the room.

That's not the Duke of Hartwell I remember. The gentleman he recalled was older than his father and occasionally had dealings with them.

Lord Spalding introduced the duke to the company.

He must be the son. Kenneth had heard there was one, Richard Jarvis, Earl of Manton. *Perhaps the father died, and this man inherited Hartwell and the dukedom.*

Lord Eamon stood and nodded. "Your Grace, we're honored by your visit."

"Thank you for inviting me, Lord Eamon. Lord Spalding has always spoken highly of you and your daughter, Miss Tarleton. Please, simply address me as Duke Hartwell."

Duke Hartwell took a seat, and the company commenced eating once more.

"Is there much to care for in the wake of your father's death?" Kenneth's father asked.

Miss Tarleton glanced at Lady Jocelyn, her eyes wide and mouth ajar.

"There is," Duke Hartwell replied. "He had a brilliant steward, and his son is like him, but my father was never skilled with matters pertaining to the estate."

Kenneth's father nodded as though he knew the truth of that.

"Lady Jocelyn, it's so delightful to see you." Duke Hartwell beamed.

"Yes, it's nice to hear from you as well, at long last."

The duke appeared nonplussed for a second. "I hope we can spend some time with one another tomorrow."

"Perhaps," she replied airily.

Duke Hartwell still seemed confused as he turned his attention towards the food.

It looks like he won't make much headway with Lady Jocelyn.

The rest of dinner was interesting enough, but Kenneth was anxiously anticipating its end. He was eager for his strategy meeting with Rebecca.

*****

Rebecca

For the evening entertainment, Lord Eamon had invited a jester or funny man of sorts, and his orations were quite amusing. Rebecca could use humor. She pulled Lady Jocelyn to the side as the group made their way to the great room.

"Lord Manton's father died?" she exclaimed, trying to keep her voice down but so incredulous she couldn't help her tone. *He's Duke Hartwell now; I must remember that.*

"Yes, I thought you were aware," Lady Jocelyn said mildly.

"It never occurred to you he might be absent because he lately buried his father and inherited a dukedom?" *What is this woman all about?*

"Of course, I understand he must attend to some affairs. But he practically dropped me. I had to begin corresponding with Mr. Udayle for consolation."

Rebecca gaped at her. "You're courting two men and paying attention to Mr. Barclay? What are you doing?"

"I'm not courting Mr. Udayle. I'm simply writing for information. He and Duke Hartwell were acquainted with one another as boys, and they didn't care for each other even back then."

Rebecca digested that piece of news. *It's interesting but doesn't excuse her conduct.*

"Mr. Barclay is well aware I haven't any serious design on him," Lady Jocelyn continued. "Though I feel I'm free to develop such. I barely consider Duke Hartwell and I as courting any longer."

Rebecca narrowed her eyes.

Lady Jocelyn grinned. "This will be quite exciting. I had no idea the duke was to come. Mr. Udayle is to call upon me since he's in the area."

Rebecca sighed. "I wished you'd informed us. Father was aware of and pleased with Duke Hartwell's arrival. He'll not appreciate theatrics during his festivities."

"I would've spoken up had I known. I can speak with Lord Eamon if you wish."

Rebecca shook her head. "I'll talk to him."

"Coming into the great room?" Lady Jocelyn asked.

"I'll be there momentarily." Rebecca required some time in solitude. She was so angry with Lady Jocelyn she couldn't trust herself yet.

The quiet morning room was a soothing change. People were getting her jangled. She exhaled and closed her eyes.

Her female companionship was making the hunt complicated, not more pleasant. She was starting to regret inviting Lady Jocelyn. Rebecca would've been better off with the men at this point.

While she enjoyed being with her father's guests, she felt pressured to be lit up all the time. And there was one man in particular...

Barclay. He was another matter entirely. She used to perceive precisely what he thought of her — good or bad.

Now I don't know what to make of him.

Barclay's behavior towards her during the last twenty-four hours wasn't poor in the least, but it wasn't like how he treated other ladies either. They've been very honest and candid with one another. She never had that kind of connection with a gentleman; she didn't even have that kind of relationship with another lady friend.

"Are you unwell?" Barclay asked.

Rebecca jumped, her eyes flying open, for she hadn't heard him enter. *Take a deep breath.* "Not unwell, but unquestionably perturbed."

"You seemed distressed after you spoke with Lady Jocelyn, and I wanted to make sure you were all right." Barclay hesitated. "Are you acquainted with Duke Hartwell?"

"I am, but not deeply, and he's not what bothered me." She paused. "Were you aware that Lady Jocelyn is courting him? Or at least she was — I'm not aware of their current status."

"I had no idea."

Rebecca bit her lip. "Does that hurt or disappoint you?"

"Not at all." Barclay chuckled. "It explains why Duke Hartwell was so confused at dinner and why you looked like thunder."

"I could not believe it when I realized." She shook her head. "It's no matter."

"In light of that information, Lady Jocelyn's behavior here leaves me wondering about her character."

"I share the blame in that. It was I who suggested she come to make Duke Hartwell jealous, as she said he wasn't paying attention to her anymore."

"Lady Jocelyn is a piece of work." Barclay laughed. "And I was the perfect dupe for her plan?"

Rebecca cringed, even though his eyes were twinkling, so she knew he was in jest. "I told her not to use you."

"Did you?" Barclay took a couple of steps closer to her. "Why would you tell her that, Miss Tarleton?"

She squirmed in her seat. "Why are you calling me Miss Tarleton suddenly?"

"Is that not your name?"

"You understand my meaning."

"It's how I should address a lady, especially one of your caliber."

Rebecca's breath caught as the room filled with silence.

"You never answered my question," Barclay said.

"It's cruel to hurt you that way."

"You care that much?"

Rebecca looked away. "I don't want anyone cruelly hurt."

"Of course. But given your opinion of me and my behavior towards you, I could see you wanting to humble me. And it wouldn't have been undeserved."

"Not in that manner," said Rebecca quietly.

"Is that the only reason?"

Rebecca stared at her hands.

"I hope there's another reason," he said.

"What reason do you wish?"

"I'd wish you'd want me for yourself."

Rebecca tried to tamp down her giddiness. *I do, but as he said, his behavior towards me has been wanting. I'll not make it easy for him.* "We should strategize."

"We should finish this conversation."

"Is there more you want to share?"

"You never said how you felt."

"You didn't ask, and you never expressed how you felt, only what you wished from me. Frankly, given your feelings a few weeks ago, one might question why you inquired. What if I don't want you?"

Barclay's face fell. "So you don't?"

"I didn't say one way or the other. My query was a hypothetical one."

He exhaled. "You drive me to insanity."

"That's the path to a lady's affections, Barclay."

"In every way possible," he continued. "I wake up in the morning now wondering if you slept well. Fight with you constantly, simultaneously wishing it would end, but desiring it'll go on because, for that bit of time, I have your undivided attention. I fume over the argument because you're always right, and then I feel guilty because you are right, and I've fallen short. Rebecca, please, please court me. I realize I should be the last man you'd want to court because I've treated you so poorly. But I'm desperately hoping you're willing to see past all the idiot things I say and do to find something good that might sway you to take a chance. And if I mess it up, you can toss me out—"

"Barclay, yes."

"What?"

His rambling speech reminded her of a tremendous reason why she liked him. He had his faults, but he was working on them. So many never do.

She smiled warmly at him. "I'll court you. I've been waiting for ages to hear that question from you."

"Truly?" He sounded amazed. "Lady Jocelyn intimated that you might be inclined towards me, but I put little store by that."

"I need a new companion. You've never guessed?"

"I had no idea. We were always arguing. And when we weren't, it seemed as though you were laughing at me."

"There were times when you were quite comical. Just because I fancied you didn't mean I didn't see you."

The two held a gaze.

"Unless you're more inclined to take me on the voyage, we should get to work," Rebecca said, breaking the hold. "Or we could hear the orator."

Barclay sat in front of her. "I like it in here with you better."

Rebecca flushed. "Good. I may try to cut Lady Jocelyn out of the deal."

"I have no problems leaving her behind, and I'm still not taking you, so prepare yourself for the challenge."

The two grinned at one another again. Barclay leaned towards Rebecca, and her eyes drifted close.

The door to the morning room flew open, and Lord Eamon poked his head in.

Rebecca and Barclay jumped apart.

"I wondered where you two had gone," Lord Eamon said.

Rebecca cleared her throat. "We're strategizing for tomorrow, Papa."

"Right. If it were anyone other than Kenneth, we'd be having a chat now. We're almost done, so if you two could wrap up your so-called strategizing, Percival would like to get back." Rebecca's father left the room.

"That was awkward," Barclay said. "I would've preferred to speak with him before he saw anything."

"I'll talk to him tonight. I'd like to tell him."

"Then I'll formally request an audience with him in the morning." He paused. "I never know if your father likes me or not."

"He finds great amusement in teasing you." Her face softened. "But in some respects, I think he looks upon you as a son."

*****

Later that night, Rebecca entered the library.

"You have news for me, daughter?" her father asked gently.

She beamed. "I do, but before I share it, I want to make you aware that Lady Jocelyn may entertain a visitor over the next couple of days. A Mr. Quentin Udayle."

"Lady Jocelyn seems to be collecting a number of gentleman callers. Do I need to be wary of this Quentin Udayle? Will he cause trouble?"

"Based on what I observed of him in London, I'd say no. But he and Duke Hartwell were romantic rivals for Lady Jocelyn during the spring, and apparently, they've been adversaries of one sort or another since childhood."

Her father frowned. "Thank you for the information. I'll put the servant staff on alert. I don't want my guests disturbed, and that includes Duke Hartwell. Lord Spalding requested his inclusion, but I issued the invitation personally." He paused. "Your choice of companionship is interesting."

"I thought she was more ladylike. I wanted to study her example."

"You keep mentioning being ladylike." Papa's brow wrinkled. "I'm at a loss as to what you believe that means. I've repeatedly stated you're a fine woman. What on earth would you learn from her?"

Rebecca played with her hands.

"So tell me, did Kenneth get himself out of the past?" her father inquired.

"He asked to court me, and I accepted."

"Finally," Papa muttered.

"You noticed his partiality? Lord Putnam did as well."

"It noticed on our last visit to Archer Hall," her father replied. "I knew Kenneth was sweet on Miss Northrop, or Lady Corwyn now, and I couldn't blame him. But even then, something was simmering under the surface between you and him. I was confident of

Kenneth's feelings, but less sure of yours and also uncertain if Kenneth would act on his."

"Do you disapprove?"

"Not at all. Despite his bumbling and, occasionally, insolent manner, he's a congenial and creditable man at heart, and I've always liked his earnestness."

Rebecca nodded vigorously. "Me too."

"For whatever reason, it's taking a long time for Kenneth to come into his own, but he's finally getting there. I told his father not to be so harsh on him, but patience isn't a quality in which he excels. So Percival spoke with you? What did he have to say?"

"He sought my patience with his son."

Her father laughed heartily. "Percival has always held you in high esteem, ever since you were a little girl. You do know how extraordinary it is for a man like him to beg your pardon for his son?"

Rebecca pulled on a curl. She'd never thought of it in that light, but she supposed it was very different.

"He's absolutely right. He and Kenneth should come begging for you."

Rebecca hugged and kissed her father goodnight.

CHAPTER 17

The Strategy

Kenneth

"We need another strategy session." Kenneth grinned at Rebecca the following morning as he sat beside her in the great room. "We didn't have a real one last night, so it needs to be a long session with a considerable amount of practice afterward."

Rebecca chuckled. "You'll hear no complaints from me."

They ate breakfast and then went for a ride before practicing.

As they took a rest by a stream in the woods, Rebecca appraised Kenneth. "You seem so comfortable out here, yet this place has only lately become your home."

"I did grow up near timberland, though I prefer this piece of country. Our forests are dense and dark, like Archer Hall. These woods are airy and pretty, like Laidley Park. And they're near you."

Rebecca smiled.

"I recognize it's quite different for you, but you're still here, enjoying it," Kenneth remarked. "How did you do it?"

"I'm not sure I have completely." She sat next to him and laid her head on his shoulder. "But I know the forest better, and Papa prepared me like a wilderness warrior." Rebecca repositioned herself and showed Kenneth her holster underneath her jacket.

His eyes grew wide. "Do you always wear that?"

"Only when I come out here."

"I'm sure your father was terrified when he couldn't find you."

Rebecca nodded. "When he finally did, it was one of the few times I've seen him cry."

Kenneth took her hand, and they sat in silence for a bit.

"A few weeks ago, I was questioning you about why you were with Lord Spencer in the woods unchaperoned," Kenneth said wryly.

"You're no Lord Spencer." Rebecca stood. "But you raise a good point. We should return."

Thirty minutes later, they were in the morning room studying the course layout with Baxter and Spalding.

"Where do you think your father will lay the targets?" Baxter asked her.

She bit her lip. "He likes challenges, surprises, and sport, so he'll probably put one by the bend in the creek or even on the other side."

"I half expect him to have a dummy drop out of a tree or pop up from the ground," said Spalding.

Baxter chuckled. "Do us in by fright."

"There are a few straight stretches," Spalding commented. "You don't think he'll put any there? Too easy?"

"He might, due to the variety of skill levels present," Rebecca answered. "He wishes the events to be enjoyable for all."

"That may be a fitting spot for several in quick succession," Kenneth said.

"Excellent thought," agreed Rebecca.

Spalding clapped Baxter on the back. "Let's ride the course."

The two men left the room.

"Splendid idea." Rebecca jumped up.

"We can give them a head start," Kenneth said.

"So we're to walk real slow."

"I have a better idea." He took her hand. "Can I give you a sweet peck? I like it when you talk strategy."

"You're very strange, but at least I can do that naturally."

"That's what I like about it." A peck was about all he had time for when the door flew open.

"Rebecca!" her father called.

She jumped and screamed, knocking Kenneth on the forehead.

Rebecca gave his chin a light rub and whirled around. "Papa, you never come in here."

He was chuckling. "Which is why you felt free to be smooching."

Rebecca turned as red as her hair.

"Lady Jocelyn is searching for you," Lord Eamon said.

"Then it's good she hasn't found me."

"You invited her here," her father chided.

She sighed. "I know, but could you not volunteer that you discovered me?"

"Are you serious?" Lord Eamon asked.

Rebecca grabbed Kenneth's hand. "I want one drama-free day with Barclay."

"All right, but if she asks outright, I'm telling her where I saw you."

"Then we won't tell you where we're going." She dragged Kenneth out of the room.

*****

Rebecca

Rebecca and Barclay caught up to Lord Spalding and Mr. Baxter on the course, and the four of them rode at a slow canter.

She was having difficulty concentrating.

"Miss Tarleton?" asked Lord Spalding.

Rebecca jerked her head towards him. "Did you ask me something?"

"Yes, twice. What happened to you? You were clear as a bell in the morning room, and now you're in some other world."

Barclay smirked.

That snapped her out of it. *He needn't look so proud of himself.* "My apologies. I was contemplating ways Barclay could improve his technique."

"What's wrong with it?" he asked, sounding defensive.

"We should work on your aim."

"It's not as though I missed."

"But Miss Tarleton is always dead-on," said Lord Spalding. "You might learn a few things from her."

"How would you know?" Barclay challenged.

Lord Spalding gave him an odd expression. "We were all there."

Barclay's jaw dropped, and then he nodded. "The hunt. Exactly. She's always dead-on."

"What did you think I was talking about?" Lord

Spalding asked.

Baxter snorted.

Lord Spalding studied Rebecca and Barclay for a moment and then laughed. "You two can continue that conversation later."

Barclay looked annoyed. "The course."

"Yes, of course. Your aim." Lord Spalding chortled as they approached one of the straightaways.

"If this is one of the rapid-fire target spots, perhaps Miss Tarleton should take it." Baxter gave Barclay a sly look. "Since you need to improve your aim."

"Rapid-fire could be terrifying," Lord Spalding chimed in. "Never know where it'd land. Knock a lady right out."

Baxter let out a shriek of laughter.

"I'll have you know she was the one who knocked me on the forehead," Barclay said.

"Barclay!" Rebecca exclaimed.

"Forehead?" Lord Spalding asked. "It's worse than I thought."

"I suppose if you overshot the approach," began Baxter as he made arcing motions with his hand.

"But then his chin would hit her head," Lord Spalding continued, "not the other way around—"

"Could we please stop!" *The ridiculousness.*

Lord Spalding cleared his throat. "Of course, I apologize, Miss Tarleton. I get carried away."

"Was that a not-so-subtle hint to refrain from kissing you?" Barclay asked later on as they rode towards the house. The other two men had gone ahead of them.

"No, I didn't think the conversation would get out of hand. You looked so smug, and it irked me."

"I can't be proud that I made a great lady like you forget herself?"

Rebecca grinned.

"But now you've made me doubt myself."

"We could practice so you can gain your confidence back."

"Excellent. Let's hurry and return."

After they returned the horses, Barclay pulled her inside the house. "Should we try the morning room—"

"Kenneth!" Papa called.

Barclay halted. "Yes?"

Papa walked up to them with a mischievous expression. "Was I interrupting anything?"

"Not at all, Lord Eamon. We're heading towards the great room to join everyone there."

"I thought I heard plans for the morning room."

"Well, people could be there too," Barclay responded. "But we're going to the great room."

"Wonderful. So am I." Papa put an arm around Kenneth's shoulder, and the two headed towards the great room.

Rebecca shook her head and followed.

CHAPTER 18

Discordant Harmony

Kenneth

"Mr. Barclay, may I have a moment's discourse with you?" Lady Jocelyn asked early Monday morning.

Kenneth had awakened excited with anticipation, so he rode ahead of Notley and his father, arriving at Stoddard Grove earlier than usual. "What would you like to discuss?"

"Let's speak outside," suggested Lady Jocelyn. "Perhaps a turn in the gardens."

Now what's happening?

Once they were on the grounds, Lady Jocelyn asked, "I realize this is unusual for a lady to ask, but could I persuade you to court me?"

Rebecca never told her? "I must politely decline that request."

Lady Jocelyn heaved an enormous sigh. "Then I don't know what I shall do. Duke Hartwell and I were courting, and he practically dropped me. As a desperate move, I hoped to make him jealous by being with you."

Kenneth fought to keep his eyes from rolling. *How did Rebecca befriend her?* Though he'd considered her a model lady when he'd first met her too. "I'm sorry to hear about your disappointment, but I'm courting Miss Tarleton."

Lady Jocelyn stopped short. "I'm quite astonished."

"Two days ago, you believed I was taken with her."

"But I never imagined you'd want to attach yourself to her, unless this courtship is solely to amuse yourself. You would have a lot of fun with Miss Tarleton."

"I don't amuse myself with young women, Lady Jocelyn."

"If you weren't courting her, would you have considered my request?" she asked, starting to walk again. "As helping a lady in need?"

"No."

"Why ever not?"

"If we were courting, I'd feel it necessary to slumber with one eye open."

Lady Jocelyn let out a peal of laughter. "And yet Miss Tarleton is the woman who can use a pistol. I'm surprised you provoke her as much as you do."

"At the end of the day, she's steadfast. I suspect you'd sacrifice me in a second."

"Hmm, there's probably some truth in that. I suppose there's no way to persuade you then?"

"None."

"Well, there's always Mr. Udayle. He'd be more than willing to oblige."

"There's no Mr. Udayle here."

"He's to call upon me since everyone is busy doing their things."

Kenneth gave her a look.

"I should be allowed to amuse myself with other company as well," she replied. "The rest of you might barely know he's here."

"I'm certain you'll ensure that doesn't occur," Kenneth muttered.

Lady Jocelyn grinned. "You're not acquainted with Mr. Udayle?"

Kenneth shook his head.

"He's the right-hand man of Lord Broughton and the mill he owns. If you're seeking people to use your ship once it's built, you might develop an in there."

Ordinarily, Kenneth would key in on that suggestion, but since it came from Lady Jocelyn, he was wary. She'd been trying to exploit him for their entire brief acquaintance, and there was little reason to believe it would cease now.

"I'll bear that in mind," he said.

"I could arrange an introduction."

"I'm currently working with Lord Spalding, and Duke Hartwell has expressed an interest through him. In the short term, I'll work with them until I'm more established."

"Very well, but I'd keep my options open."

More like keep my eyes open.

✱✱✱✱✱

Rebecca

Rebecca paused on the stairs as she watched Barclay come in with Lady Jocelyn. She was eager to see Barclay and go over the plan one more time before the competition, but that sight stopped her dead in her tracks.

I hate being possessive or constantly suspicious, but what are they doing walking together? She hadn't told Lady Jocelyn she and Barclay were courting, but he certainly knew.

Rebecca waited for them to pass before she finished her descent. She didn't feel like putting on pretenses and wished to remain in the euphoria she'd experienced Saturday night and Sunday. Rebecca also sought to keep her composure for today's challenge. The scores were close, so she needed an excellent performance to maintain her presence in the competition. The men had been good about not looking down upon her, but she wanted to assert her dominance regardless.

Barclay sat beside her at breakfast, smiling broadly, and asked how she slept.

Rebecca tried to respond as though nothing were vexing her.

He wrinkled his brow. "Are you ill?"

"No, I'm well in body."

"How about in mind and spirit?"

"I suppose I could be more settled there."

"I'm sure you'll perform prodigiously. You've always put in a strong showing."

Rebecca gave him what she hoped was a grateful smile. "Thank you."

She didn't engage him in further conversation, and her responses to his questions were short. After breakfast, they headed to the competition area together and discussed the strategy once more along the way.

Barclay suddenly halted. "Are you upset with me, Rebecca?"

"It'll pass," she replied.

"What have I done?"

"It's nothing to discuss now."

"Besides the fact that I don't want you upset with me, any rift between us will decrease the quality of our performance. Please tell me what's wrong."

Rebecca sighed. "You seem friendlier with Lady Jocelyn than necessary."

"I believe I'm less friendly towards her than the others."

"So you always embark on early morning strolls with the fellows?" She didn't intend to sound sarcastic, but Barclay's tone was dismissive again, and that invariably set her on edge.

He narrowed his eyes. "She asked, and I saw no reason to decline. It was a walk. Why would that agitate you?"

"Because you were partial towards her when she first arrived."

"I'm courting you now."

Rebecca raised an eyebrow.

Barclay exhaled. "She was pleasing to the eyes, and I wasn't immune to her flattery, but I set no serious store by her."

"She could easily change your mind."

"Why are you so insecure?"

"Why are you so careless?"

The two glared at one another as the others entered the field.

"We need to work this out, or it'll degrade our performance," Barclay said.

Rebecca scoffed. "Speak for yourself. I always rise to the challenge. I'll replay your words whenever I aim for the target."

"You're ridiculous."

"And you're dismissive. I told you before I won't stand for that."

Lord Eamon called the group to order.

*****

Kenneth

Kenneth and Rebecca drew the last spot, which made for an uncomfortable wait period. Lord Eamon would ride a parallel course so he could watch the pairs along with the servant teams stationed at each test. Fortunately, he didn't seem aware of any tension and was more excited for this challenge than the contestants. Kenneth's father gave him and Rebecca a couple of curious looks, but thankfully, he went second after Spalding and Baxter, so Kenneth escaped questioning.

Repington snickered at Kenneth after Lord Putnam and Notley set off. "Were you too familiar with Miss Rebecca again?"

"You're not helping," Kenneth grumped.

"You seem to have a knack for putting your foot in it," Repington teased. "Spalding shares that same gift. Perhaps you two could discuss your differing styles."

Fitzpatrick chuckled.

Repington sobered. "An apology goes a long way."

"Why does everyone assume it's my fault?" Kenneth retorted.

Repington threw him a bemused look.

"I hardly know for what I'm apologizing," muttered Kenneth.

"Do you need to?" Fitzpatrick asked.

Kenneth regarded him, surprised. Fitzpatrick seldom spoke. "How else am I to apologize?"

"I'd think it'd be better to focus on restoring the peace rather than who's right or wrong," Fitzpatrick answered. "If the issue is even that black and white."

Kenneth mulled that over. It was an interesting line of thought, though he wasn't sure how it applied regarding Rebecca.

"So Fitz, you have much experience along these lines?" Repington asked. "I have difficulty imagining you arguing with anyone."

"On the contrary, I assure you. I've had my share of arguments and never courted a woman in my life."

Kenneth was shocked, for Fitzpatrick was a man of means with excellent connections and well-favored.

"You commented I possess impossibly high standards, and yet you never liked a lady."

"I said courted, Barclay," Fitzpatrick repeated.

"Ah," Kenneth replied, finally understanding. "Surely, you'll win her in the end."

"It'd help if I didn't have to win her affection away from my brother," Fitzpatrick remarked dryly.

"Oh." The other two men exchanged glances.

Lord Eamon returned. "Pair three is up next."

Fitzpatrick and Repington took off. Kenneth rode closer to Rebecca as he and the other gentlemen had been apart from her and Mr. Adams.

Fortunately, Mr. Adams was affable and conversational as usual, so Rebecca and Kenneth spoke with him instead of interacting with one another.

Their turn came about twenty minutes later.

"Get us our win!" cheered Mr. Adams.

They were off. The course resembled a needle with a circular hole — the beginning and end straightaways with a wide loop in the middle. Rebecca rode to the left where the fields were and Barclay to the right with trees. The contest had a tame beginning, each taking two marks on their own sides. The path turned, and a grassy field opened up on the right with five targets in a row.

That'll be tight.

Rebecca whipped out her arrows. "I got it."

They crisscrossed.

She hit every one of them and a bullseye for two.

Rebecca is relentless.

The path bent right, and Kenneth could narrowly make out the stream ahead.

"Duck," Rebecca commanded.

Kenneth dodged an arrow shot over him, striking a target he never noticed to his left, installed on a large rock outcropping. She scored a nine.

The stream curved.

There it is. Barclay took aim and hit the target across the water.

"Excellent shot," Rebecca surged forward.

An object dropped from a tree, and she rode through it.

"Barclay!" she yelled as she cut left.

"I'm here." He barely got the arrow off, but the profusion of feathers indicated he struck something. He fanned a few away from his face. Lord Eamon had a ridiculous sense of humor, though they had anticipated this. It was a wonder the horses didn't get spooked.

"Fence," he called. It wasn't large, as there was space on either end to avoid it if the rider wanted.

Rebecca cut in and rode close, and they jumped it simultaneously.

A target approached on his side and then hers that they each took. Then one appeared dead center. They both shot at it. Rebecca bullseye. Barclay nine.

Rebecca was unstoppable, but to Kenneth's surprise, he put on a solid performance as well.

Lord Eamon met them at the finish. "I don't wish to play favorites, but it was a joy watching you two complete that course. Like a dance. Beautiful harmony. Nice job."

Rebecca and Barclay exchanged uneasy looks.

"I'm heading in to join the others," she said quietly and rode off.

Barclay sighed. He was the last to enter the great room. There weren't any free seats in the circle, so he walked towards Baxter on the couch and waved his arm, asking him to move over.

"Do I resemble Miss Tarleton?" Baxter quipped.

"Shove over." Barclay slid into the seat.

Lord Eamon announced the results. Rebecca won, and the two of them as a team came in first place.

Kenneth feared he'd have to figure out a way to sail with her. If she ever talked to him again.

It was hard to be agreeable for the rest of the afternoon. Kenneth couldn't stop his mind from straying towards Rebecca, and she kept her distance from him.

He didn't understand why she was so upset with him. He had no feelings for Lady Jocelyn. On the contrary, he found her a bit of an irritant now. Rebecca was being irrational, or she was used to unending devotion and attention from her suitors. This whole situation was ludicrous.

He felt that pricking of foreboding. Rebecca had accused him of dismissing her.

Can I see her more clearly?

Rebecca gave him the deep freeze again during dinner when he tried to engage her in light conversation and then announced she'd retire early due to a headache.

Lady Jocelyn sat next to him in the great room after Rebecca left. "My offer is still on the table." She chuckled.

Kenneth glared at her.

"I figured as much, but thought I'd give it a go anyway," Lady Jocelyn replied. "I realize you two were always arguing, but it seems a bit early in your courtship to have a disagreement so large."

"I'm at a loss as to my transgression. You're part of the problem."

"What did I do?"

"She must have seen us return from our walk and jumped to conclusions."

"She's never been that sensitive before. She must actually be in love with you."

"Why is she so absurd about this? I don't like you."

Lady Jocelyn snorted.

"I apologize; that was coarse."

"Whether or not you feel it's rational, it's her feelings. And if you are to keep her now that you've secured her affection, you'll have to take those seriously."

It's odd that she and Fitzpatrick would travel a similar line of reasoning. "Ironic you're instructing me on how to treat her properly when you've been less than diligent in that yourself."

"Yes, well, it's not as though I don't like Miss Tarleton. I do. But her goals interfered with mine, so I needed to do something about that temporarily."

Kenneth shook his head.

"She's not completely incorrect," Lady Jocelyn commented. "I did ask you to court me during that walk."

"But I flat out rejected it, and you sought me solely to incite Duke Hartwell."

"I wouldn't have appealed to a man for whom I had no attraction, and despite your feelings for me now, you were attracted to me when we were first acquainted."

Kenneth looked away.

"Don't be so dismissive, and actually listen and attempt to understand her. It's a wonder she likes you at all the way you treat her sometimes. You must have great potential."

"And I'm the coarse one?" He asked with a raised eyebrow.

Lady Jocelyn offered him a slight shrug and walked away.

CHAPTER 19

Mr. Udayle

Rebecca

Rebecca lay in her bed the next morning, not wanting to be in company. Tuesday was another rest day.

She heard Barclay's words in her mind for the hundredth time. *'Why are you so insecure?'*

I am unsteady in myself. I don't know how to alter that. I just am. But I don't want that to drive him away either.

Rebecca rolled over. I can't stay in bed. I must be a hostess — rest day or not.

She went downstairs after dressing, and the first person she saw was Barclay. It appeared he had recently arrived with his father and Mr. Notley.

He seemed tentative. "Good morning, Rebecca. Would you favor me with a ride?"

Rebecca contemplated him as his father and Mr. Notley walked away.

"Please," he begged. "I want to apologize, but I also believe there are a couple of matters we need to discuss."

She nodded. "I'll get my things."

Rebecca was about to leave her quarters again when the housekeeper entered. "Mr. Udayle has arrived, and Lady Jocelyn is with him in the drawing room."

She sighed. *As if there wasn't enough occurring.* "Thank you."

Rebecca raced downstairs. "Can we put off our ride?" she asked Barclay. "Lady Jocelyn has a guest that I want to be present for."

"I think that's a wise idea."

"You know Mr. Udayle?"

"No, but Lady Jocelyn was anxious for me to meet him, which makes me suspicious. May I accompany you?"

"Of course," Rebecca replied. "Do you wish to become acquainted with him?"

"I believe, in this case, some information would be more advantageous than being completely in the dark."

They went to the drawing room and joined the other two guests.

Slender with sharp features, Mr. Quentin Udayle had a compelling presence. He seemed watchful and reminded Rebecca of a hawk. He was comely, but his countenance came across more severe than many gentlemen his age. Rebecca had thought Duke Hartwell the pleasanter of the two men, but Mr. Udayle possessed a flair for the dark and dramatic, which was captivating in its own way and would appeal to Lady Jocelyn.

"Mr. Barclay, you're gaining some attention," Mr. Udayle said. "The gentleman who builds speedy ships. When it seemed like a hobby, nobody took notice, but now that you're working with Lord Spalding, there's been more talk. Have you considered going into textiles?"

"Not in detail, no."

"You should. It's lucrative."

"Mr. Yeatman and a couple of his associates command a lock on that," Barclay noted.

"True," Mr. Udayle conceded. "But I'm sure there are those that would like to cultivate other options if possible."

"I obviously want my vessel used, but currently, I'm focused on building the craft itself and working with Lord Spalding. It's already a new arena for me."

"I understand," Mr. Udayle replied. "Keep Lord Broughton and me in mind. You'd have a listening ear."

"All this business talk," huffed Lady Jocelyn. "I thought you came to call upon me, Mr. Udayle?"

"I won't let anything else distract me from that delightful task. What would you like to do?"

"What would you suggest?" Lady Jocelyn asked Rebecca. "We are quite in the wilderness out here."

It is the country. "If you'd prefer to take a carriage ride, I can arrange that," Rebecca offered. "It might be a little more comfortable than being out of doors on foot."

"Excellent. Would you two care to join us?" Mr. Udayle asked.

"We had our own horseback ride planned," Barclay answered. "But I'll inquire if one of the other guests would accompany you."

"Thank you. We'd appreciate that," said Lady Jocelyn.

Barclay and Rebecca left the drawing room a few minutes later, and Rebecca made the arrangements for the carriage ride.

"Who do you suppose would go with them?" Rebecca asked Barclay.

"Most of the other's opinions aren't as strong as ours. The larger complication will be who's still here."

Mr. Notley and Repington were playing billiards but said they'd be happy to take a break and accompany Lady Jocelyn and Mr. Udayle.

The group was in the entranceway when Duke Hartwell walked through. "Mr. Udayle. I didn't realize you were here for this event."

Rebecca exhaled. *I was hoping to avoid this.*

Lady Jocelyn practically glowed.

"I've come for the day to call upon Lady Jocelyn," answered Mr. Udayle. "Her correspondence sounded as though she could use a little company."

Duke Hartwell's face grew dark. "And I'm here to provide it."

"But you were away for so long," said Lady Jocelyn. "I couldn't bear it anymore."

"The time was not lengthy, and we spent the last two days together," Duke Hartwell said. "I was endeavoring to rush matters so we could return to the way things were, but there's been so much to do regarding the estate."

He shouldn't feel guilty. "I'm sure everyone here understands the great strain you must bear due to your father's death."

"Thank you," he replied.

Mr. Udayle offered Lady Jocelyn his arm. "We should take our ride." As Lady Jocelyn took it, Mr. Udayle looked towards Barclay. "And I hope we'll hear from you in the future when you're ready to ship textiles."

Duke Hartwell glanced at Barclay sharply.

There's a game afoot, and somehow Barclay seems to have landed smack in the middle of it. Again.

"You're to do business with Udayle and Broughton?" Duke Hartwell asked Barclay when the foursome had departed.

"The only person I have an agreement with is Spalding," Barclay replied.

"But you're considering others?" Duke Hartwell pressed. "Spalding spoke to you of my plans and wishes?"

"In a general manner, yes, he did." Barclay paused. "Duke Hartwell, if you would please excuse us, I asked Miss Tarleton for a ride, quite some time ago, as we must discuss a pressing matter. Can we postpone our conversation about shipping until perhaps tomorrow?"

"Of course. I didn't realize." He grimaced. "Mr. Udayle's appearance threw me completely off."

"We apologize for that," Rebecca said. "We weren't aware he was coming until a day ago, and it was by Lady Jocelyn's invitation."

"I hope it didn't inconvenience you," Duke Hartwell said.

"We were only concerned for the comfort of our invited guests," Rebecca assured him.

"Thank you. I'll let the two of you attend to your outing." The duke walked off.

"I reckon we can finally take our ride," Barclay said.

CHAPTER 20

Diversions

Rebecca

Rebecca's and Barclay's horses walked at a slow gait on the path of the course track from the previous day. *Even when there was tension between us, we still worked well together. Imagine what we could do as a united team.*

"What goods were Lord Spalding interested in shipping?" she asked Barclay.

"He spoke primarily of cocoa and spices, but not in huge quantities, and I'm unclear as to how much money he'll actually make. I think it's a novelty to him, and he wants chocolate."

Barclay is more candid about this than I expected. "You told Mr. Udayle you hadn't thought about textile in detail. But you've considered it?"

"Lord Spalding said Duke Hartwell inquired after steamships. He's working with Lord Thurston, and there's a possibility some of that could come my way."

Rebecca raised her eyebrows. "Thurston? He's becoming a great mogul of textile."

"Yes, though I believe he's to keep within England, Scotland, and Wales. You're aware of that?"

"I own shares in his millworks."

"Your nest egg is decent then. You're more actively involved than I realized."

"Father thought I should understand its management, and I took off with it."

"Apparently." Barclay seemed impressed. "Lord Thurston has recently made improvements to his mill, which already increased his production."

"It appears you may land in the midst of a tug-o-war."

"I got that sense too."

They rode in silence a bit.

"Are you truly bothered by my talking to Lady Jocelyn?" Barclay asked gently.

Rebecca sighed. "Yes. A part of me says I shouldn't, especially after what just happened, but I am. I can't explain it."

"I'll be careful with her. As you pointed out, I was drawn to her when she first arrived, so your feelings have some foundation."

"Thank you."

"And even if they didn't, I still shouldn't dismiss your concerns. I'm sorry."

"I am as well. I know you don't like Lady Jocelyn. I'll work harder at being less..." Rebecca trailed off at a loss for words.

"Be Rebecca," Barclay said. "You're fine the way you are." He smiled at her. "I was slow to admit how much I admire it."

Fine the way I am. Rebecca's heart melted.

The two rode in silence for a bit.

"I propose you and I have a diversion day," Barclay declared.

Rebecca grinned. "And what does that entail?"

"When I have one with my sisters, we don't take our meals in the dining room, and we eat our favorite foods whenever we want. Play games and go for rides like we're doing now. I'd imagine your brand might be a little different."

"I liked everything you suggested. But let's tweak it a bit."

*****

Kenneth

Kenneth grasped the edge of the conveyance. "This wasn't the kind of ride I had envisioned."

Spalding gave a whoop on the other side of Rebecca, the three squashed into her new phaeton that her father had bought her. "I can't believe Lord Eamon got you one of these. I've been eyeing a similar model myself. It's amazing how fast you can go and still feel stable."

"Stable?" Kenneth exclaimed.

"I've never gone at this speed before!" Rebecca exclaimed.

Kenneth groaned.

"This'll be the last time I can take it out for a while," Rebecca commented. "We're fortunate the roads are good." She glanced at Barclay. "I better slow down. Barclay is turning pale."

Kenneth gave her a look. "Where is it you mentioned we were tearing off to?"

"The village down the road," Rebecca replied. "Pratts has the best ale, pudding, and meat pies. We can stuff ourselves and bring some back for later."

"You're taking us to a tavern?" Kenneth asked incredulously.

Rebecca rolled her eyes. "You forget where you are. It's a room built on the side of an elderly widow's house. You men are rowdier in the great room than it ever gets at Mrs. Pratts."

"Then to Pratts we shall go."

A few hours later, Kenneth's dart went very high when the trio played in the gentlemen's room.

"You're astonishingly bad at this," Rebecca remarked.

He shrugged. "I rarely play this game."

Kenneth was enjoying himself anyway. He meant it when he told Rebecca to be herself, and Kenneth could do the same with her. She'd tell him straight away if there was an issue, and they could iron matters out. It felt good to be unburdened and stabilized in such a manner.

Spalding stretched. "It's been most entertaining, but time I sought the bed."

Kenneth pulled Rebecca close to him after Spalding had left the room. "Did you enjoy yourself today?"

"I had a marvelous time. You?"

"Yes, I loved being with you." His lips had scarcely grazed hers when he heard a throat clear behind him and whirled around.

"Hi, Papa." Rebecca giggled. "We were saying goodnight."

Kenneth cringed. *Why is he always catching me with her?*

"Since that's been thoroughly covered, everyone can go to bed." Lord Eamon said dryly. "Kenneth, your father and Mr. Notley are waiting for you in the great room."

"Right, good night, Lord Eamon." Kenneth walked past him and then glanced back at Rebecca.

She beamed at him.

I'll sleep very well tonight.

CHAPTER 21

The Scavenger Hunt

Kenneth

"A scavenger hunt is a fun play on the hunt," Spalding said the following day. Their team gathered at the far end of the great room by the billiards table, along with Lady Jocelyn and Duke Hartwell.

"Five clues. Five of us," Mr. Adams said. "Would everyone rather remain together as a group or take clues individually?"

"Let's try individually," suggested Baxter. "We'll finish faster. If it appears better to be paired once we read them, we can change."

"Very good. There's another set of clues at the spots where we find these items?" asked Mr. Adams.

"Correct," confirmed Spalding.

"Mr. Barclay, I'd like to accompany you if you're agreeable," said Duke Hartwell.

"Absolutely," Kenneth replied. "It'd be a pleasure."

"Lady Jocelyn, you're free to come with any of us or, of course, Miss Tarleton," said Baxter.

"Thank you. It's kind of you to think of that since others did not." Lady Jocelyn glared at Duke Hartwell.

"My apologies," Duke Hartwell said. "I assumed you've been accompanying Miss Tarleton. I wish to talk a bit of business with Mr. Barclay, but I'm yours after the scavenger hunt."

Lady Jocelyn exhaled. "If it must be."

"Lord Eamon," the butler called from the door. "Miss Ada Adams is here again. She says she has muffins for the company."

Lord Eamon laughed. "Adams, your girl knows she's unlikely to find a husband here, right?"

Mr. Adams groaned. "I'll speak with her. Lady Jocelyn, would you be so kind as to favor me with your presence? It might give my advice some weight."

"I'd be happy to oblige, Mr. Adams," she replied.

"Make sure you bring back the muffins," Baxter called after them. "They're excellent," he said to the others. "We can't allow that goodness go to waste."

The rest of them each took a clue, and after deciding the tasks could be easily completed as individuals, they dispersed.

"The kitchen staff should have a bone," Kenneth commented to Duke Hartwell.

As they made their way to the kitchen, the duke asked with a mouthful of muffin, "You're interested in building steamships?"

Kenneth hesitated. "I am. What's your interest in steam?"

"It sounds like the next major advancement, and if you have devices involved that can be patented and sold—"

"Not yet. I'm working on my human talent right now."

"Understandable." He glanced downward. "This is tasty. I wonder how she gets them so moist."

Kenneth gave him a curious look.

"Right. Steamships." Duke Hartwell popped the last piece into his mouth and brushed his hands together. "I ask because I'm currently collaborating with Lord Thurston on his mill expansion, and faster freight would dovetail well."

Lord Thurston's move to break ties with an established shipping giant and try a new, untested one was gutsy. Almost reckless in Kenneth's mind, but since he was the one who was being tested, his opinion wasn't as severe.

Kenneth made his request to the kitchen head, and she gifted him with a good-sized bone, as well as their next clue.

"It appears we'll be outside," Duke Hartwell remarked as they read.

"Are you adept at climbing trees?"

The duke grinned. "Probably as agile as you."

"This will be interesting then." A bird's nest was the most straightforward answer, but difficult to retrieve. Kenneth hoped they'd think of another solution as they searched. The day was overcast, but at least not very cold.

"I want to form a cooperation of companies," Duke Hartwell explained as they began walking across the grounds. "The Honorable English Textile Alliance or T.H.E.T.A."

"You adopt odd abbreviations," Kenneth commented. "It's quite uncommon."

"I find it diverting. Play with my words and see what hops out. I'm not skittish about working outside of convention."

Kenneth smiled. It was fortunate Duke Hartwell's rank allowed him leeway at the moment to act in such a manner. But the tide could turn against him quickly, boxing him in, and Kenneth could be swept with him.

He was wary of putting his already hemmed-in existence into further confinement.

"Each company and entity maintains its own identity, but we work together as a unit," Duke Hartwell continued. "Your ships would be a key part of the alliance."

Kenneth regarded him. "Interesting. But I don't want to promise more than I can deliver. I've exclusively built boats and have never done shipping before."

"I understand. Lord Spalding's intrigues will be a good venture to cut your teeth."

Kenneth raised an eyebrow. "Intrigues?"

"I exaggerate. But his primary interest in my project isn't to make money. He desires sweets and a place to plunk his cash."

"I'm not in that camp. I need to turn at least a little profit."

"Of course, same here. I want more than a slight profit, and you better believe Thurston does. I'd like for our group to have a company or more in each step of the textile process, so we should make good money." He paused. "That's a decent-sized tree across the lawn."

The two men headed in that direction.

"Not too many noblemen involve themselves in trade to this extent," Kenneth remarked. "We'll be in the minority. A tiny minority."

"Then we'll be our own societal division. Maybe a secret league. Shall we establish a clubhouse? How does the T.H.E.T.A. Lodge sound to you? Meeting at the THETAL has a nice ring to it. "

Kenneth shook his head, smiling. *For a serious business discussion, this is becoming a silly conversation.* "Daring isn't a word used to describe me," Kenneth said. "I'm very much mainstream and have been accused of being a man who doesn't take action."

"Here's your opportunity to change all that. I love action." The duke stopped short and pointed at the gatehouse. "There's a nest."

It was nestled between the roofline and lintel.

"You want to scale a building?" Kenneth asked, incredulous.

Duke Hartwell shrugged. "Not particularly, but it's only a single story." He took off his jacket and walked to a nearby tree. "I could probably climb the tree and get close enough to the nest." He grabbed a branch and hoisted himself up.

Kenneth's jaw dropped. "Lord Eamon will slay me if anything happens to you."

"I'm fine," the duke said after he hoisted himself onto a higher branch. "I'd invite you up here with me, but the branches might not like that."

Kenneth sighed.

"What is he doing?" Spalding said behind him.

Kenneth whirled around. "Retrieving the answer to our second clue."

"Hartwell," Spalding called up. "You should at least have an heir before you do such nonsense."

"I'm working on that." By now, Duke Hartwell was standing on one branch while holding onto the limb above. He appeared secure, but Kenneth preferred he be out of the tree as quickly as possible.

Spalding clapped Kenneth on the shoulder. "I'll leave him to you. It's nice there are enough gentlemen here to switch off monitoring him. He's quite a handful, isn't he?"

Kenneth rubbed his forehead, listening to Spalding laugh as he walked away.

"This nest is quite impressive," Duke Hartwell called down. "Must we physically present it? I feel uneasy taking a bird's home away."

Despite himself, Kenneth chuckled. "That's very thoughtful of you. Don't tell Lady Jocelyn; she might become jealous."

Duke Hartwell gave him a look.

Kenneth was surprised he was so informal with the duke. Perhaps it was because he didn't act as other men of higher nobility he'd met or seen. He came across more or less like Kenneth.

"We can fetch Lord Eamon and show him. That might be sufficient," Kenneth suggested.

"Excellent notion." In a few swift drops, Duke Hartwell was out of the tree.

Kenneth shook his head. *Definitely not like other noblemen I've met.*

As they returned to the house, Kenneth thought about the duke's offer and fought off his natural inclination to hold back because it was safe and comfortable. Inaction. It was exciting to belong to a new generation of men attempting to do things a little differently. He wasn't watching the game or doing his father's bidding. But at the same time, he didn't want to leap into anything foolish. "Are you in a viable position to take on this kind of venture?" he asked the duke. "From what I understood, you've recently assumed many responsibilities."

Duke Hartwell sobered. "I have. Let's say we all have our different outlets, and this is one of mine."

Kenneth nodded. "Spalding stated you had many pursuits, but he mentioned plants."

"Yes, that's my primary interest. But isn't it better to be varied?"

Action? Duke Hartwell is all over the place and a rather singular man, but I might enjoy riding on his coattails. "Keep me in the loop."

"Excellent! I know you're finishing the ship for Spalding. If I'm able to get Lord Thurston on board, can you build another for his line?"

Kenneth raised his eyebrows. "Why can't he be in with Spalding? From what I understood, Spalding's merchandise wasn't excessive in quantity. He wanted priority on shipping, which he wouldn't receive with Mr. Yeatman."

"Lord Thurston can share in the beginning, but I'm telling you he's exploding. We'll require another ship."

They found Lord Eamon, and talks of shipping ceased for a while as they showed him the nest. Lord Eamon was pleased that they decided not to remove it and gave them bonus points for not doing so.

"Do you need investment?" Duke Hartwell asked Kenneth after Lord Eamon left them. "I can speak with Spalding."

"I might have that covered."

"You're more tenty than you give yourself credit for."

"Let's say I know someone who prods me in that direction."

CHAPTER 22

Go After It

Kenneth

Kenneth pulled Rebecca into the morning room later that day.

"More practice?" she asked.

"We can certainly do that, but actually I have a business proposition for you. So our wager..."

She chuckled as they sat down. "It's not looking good for you, is it?"

"It's not," he conceded. "Nevertheless, I'm asking you to invest in my next project."

"Intriguing. More details, please."

Kenneth explained Duke Hartwell's plan — or vision might be more accurate. The duke hadn't propounded anything as concrete as a plan. While Kenneth used his own funds he'd saved for eons on the ship he was finishing for Spalding, between that and assuming Laidley Park, he was a touch tight right now.

"You need to think bigger, darling," Rebecca said when he finished. "I want a stake in your company."

"I don't have a company." The thought had never occurred to him. He owned property and will one day inherit a titled estate. *I preside over estates. That's what I was raised to do. I'm surrounded by people with tremendous ideas.*

"But you'd like to continue building boats and ships?" Rebecca asked.

"I would."

"And you want them to be sold and sail for you?"

"Yes."

"Then it sounds as though you're operating a business whether or not you realized it. It needn't be elaborate," Rebecca continued. "But an official shipbuilding and shipping enterprise will make your endeavors more organized. And yes, I'll invest in that in exchange for a financial stake." She regarded him with a steady expression. "If you're to do a thing, go after it."

Kenneth contemplated her. *Go after it.* "When did you metamorphose into a businesswoman?"

Rebecca shrugged. "While you weren't looking, I grew up, Barclay."

He grinned slowly. "You did indeed."

Rebecca flushed.

"I'm inclined to say you have a deal, but allow me to sleep on it," Kenneth said.

"Please do," agreed Rebecca. "And I'll require more solid plans from both you and Duke Hartwell before I hand over any money."

"Absolutely. Now, how about that practice you mentioned earlier?"

Rebecca giggled as Kenneth leaned forward.

"I'm sure they're not in the morning room," boomed Lord Eamon from the hallway.

Kenneth snatched himself away from Rebecca.

"You realize my father is aware that courting couples may exchange expressions of affection, such as kisses, with one another from time to time," she teased.

Kenneth made a face at her. "Yes, but it feels awkward for him to see me do it, especially since we're newly courting."

Rebecca shook her head and then grabbed his hand as she stood. "Come then. We might as well join everyone else in the great room."

*****

Kenneth sat at his desk wide awake again that night, playing with a miniature model of his newest ship as he contemplated the events of the last couple of days. He'd received invitations to join a group of companies and start his own. It was exciting but overwhelming. Rebecca's involvement eased some of his disquiet. Their talk helped him set his mind straight and gave him a focal point. It also imparted real courage, not the arrogant blustering he occasionally did to save face.

The model was an encouraging reminder too. *I did build a real-life one of these. I'm not completely inept.*

Rebecca was correct in saying he'd already laid the pieces in place for a company by embarking on Lord Spalding's project and building the last three boats. Organizing and making affairs official would help, not hinder, and would focus his energies better.

He smiled. *We're doing this.*

But first, they needed more information from Duke Hartwell.

*****

"What are the threats?" Rebecca asked Duke Hartwell when the three of them met together early Thursday morning.

"Threats?" Kenneth repeated.

"Any venture will have something to destroy it," Rebecca explained. "What is this venture's threat?"

"Overseas," Duke Hartwell answered.

Rebecca nodded. "There are many places that can make things cheap."

"But part of this plan was bringing operations in tighter to cut down expenses and decrease difficulties inherent with foreign ventures. It should help mitigate the risk though not eliminate it altogether." Duke Hartwell pressed his lips together. "Our largest threat is Mr. Quentin Udayle."

"How?" Kenneth asked.

Threats to the whole venture weren't something that had occurred to Kenneth. He'd been concerned with whether he could uphold his end of the agreement. And while he'd guessed Mr. Udayle could pose some kind of complication based on their brief interaction, this made it sound like he'd be a much larger problem.

Rebecca had already inquired after the other entities involved, Duke Hartwell's goals and strategy for this alliance, and the projected profit stream. She seemed comfortable with what she'd heard so far. Kenneth couldn't believe she knew to ask about those matters.

"One of our largest problems is that this is a different kind of arrangement, and it'll be difficult to sell people on that," Duke Hartwell explained. "And Mr. Udayle is a strong face for the old guard."

"He can be very persuasive." Rebecca paused. "Is the business aspect the only threat?"

"You're astute, Miss Tarleton," he replied. "But then you were with Lady Jocelyn and me in London, so you would know about that."

"I don't follow," said Kenneth.

Rebecca briefly brought Kenneth up to date on what had transpired between the two gentlemen and Lady Jocelyn in London during the past season.

"What is the matter with her?" muttered Kenneth. *That explains the confrontation in the entranceway much better.*

"Excuse me?" Duke Hartwell scrutinized him. "What is your meaning?"

Kenneth squirmed. "I meant no disrespect towards Lady Jocelyn, simply noting she seems to involve herself in many romantic entanglements."

"Do you still have an understanding with her, Duke Hartwell?" Rebecca asked carefully.

"As far as I'm concerned, I do. Why?"

"She was in a bit of doubt," Rebecca replied.

"I never indicated otherwise, verbally or by letter, and I'm here now."

"Of course," Rebecca said.

"Mr. Udayle's presence is suspect, but I can believe him worming his way in." Duke Hartwell eyed Kenneth again.

There may not have been much worming required. "Lady Jocelyn didn't make it clear to all that she wasn't free," Kenneth said tentatively.

Duke Hartwell muttered something and then glared at Kenneth. "Are you not courting Miss Tarleton?"

"That's an extremely new development," Kenneth replied.

"It's not as though Lady Jocelyn has been here long," Duke Hartwell said. "I'd say she's not the only one who gets themself into romantic entanglements."

Rebecca chuckled. "And you just know the half of it."

Kenneth scowled at her. "It's true this has not been the best of years for me."

Duke Hartwell shot him a look. "I'll speak with her as soon as possible. Again. Meanwhile, do you have any other questions or concerns for me, Miss Tarleton?"

"I want to see some of this innovation of yours, Duke Hartwell. It appears I'll personally test the ship, so I'll see the goods there."

"I heard of the little competition the two of you have going. It appears you'll be outfitting your ship with space for a lady, Mr. Barclay."

Kenneth groaned.

"And as I told Mr. Barclay, I'll need a stronger plan in writing before investing," Rebecca finished.

"Of course, we'll make sure that's provided. I'll meet with the other parties and Lady Corwyn—"

"Lady Corwyn?" Rebecca asked and exchanged looks with Kenneth.

"She's another investor and has a way with words, so she'll do much of our written correspondence and documentation," Duke Hartwell responded. "Lord Vaughnryd only agreed to participate if she was included."

"Excellent," Rebecca said. "Her involvement imparts real confidence."

Duke Hartwell chuckled. "A formal document is long overdue, so it's advantageous you're forcing us to do that. I can arrange a demonstration at your convenience."

Rebecca glanced at Kenneth.

"We'll wait until we see everything to give our final answer," Kenneth said to the duke. "But I think you might have a deal."

CHAPTER 23

Reckless Interference

Rebecca

"Chilly day for a race," commented Mr. Fitzpatrick as they assembled on the lawn an hour after Rebecca's meeting with Duke Hartwell and Barclay.

Rebecca nodded. It was November, so cooler temperatures were normal, but today was more blustery than the previous days had been. Due to the brevity of this event, they wouldn't be outside long, which pleased the younger crowd. Her father and Lord Putnam barely seemed bothered by it.

Rebecca studied Mr. Fitzpatrick. He had arresting good looks but possessed the quietest manner of everyone here, so it was easy to pass over him despite his talents and appearance. At twenty-three, he was closer to her age, but she'd always been more comfortable with his older brother, Lord Spalding.

"I must apologize, Mr. Fitzpatrick, for not visiting with you more," she said to him. "You're an able competitor, and I've enjoyed our contests together."

"Thank you, Miss Tarleton," he replied. "You as well. I wager you've had your hands full these last couple of weeks."

"True indeed," Rebecca agreed wryly.

He smiled. "Is your father's collection of guests usually this colorful?"

"No, they seem to have outdone themselves this year."

He laughed.

"I hope, despite that, you've enjoyed yourself," she said.

"Yes, absolutely. I've been enormously entertained by the company and your father's activities. He has quite the imagination and a great deal of intelligence."

"What are your plans after you leave?"

"I have none as I'm without proper occupation presently."

"Your brother seems plenty occupied. Perhaps you could find a pursuit with him?"

Mr. Fitzpatrick's face clouded over. "I could. But I rather not."

"Do you suspect something amiss with the ventures he's involved with?"

His features cleared. "No, I don't wish to alarm you in that respect. Duke Hartwell may be a little unorthodox and perhaps a bit unthinking in his actions due to his enthusiasm. But I believe the project he and my brother are connected with is essentially sound, though lacking in structure at the moment. I speak from a more personal standpoint."

Whatever is the matter between the brothers?

Her father called the company to order and broke them into two groups. Papa thought it best to separate the stronger riders so the Tarletons, Barclays, and Fitzpatrick brothers would ride in one race. The rest would be in the first group with Duke Hartwell and Lady Jocelyn.

Lord Eamon laid out another course, different from Monday's. Finishing in the top three would garner the winners and teams a tremendous amount of points, but clearing certain jumps along the way would also add bonuses.

The first group raced, and Repington, Duke Hartwell, and Notley placed.

The second group made their way to the start line.

Rebecca's competitive streak rose. She loved horse races — speed and Mason. She glanced at Barclay. *It's wonderful to race him.*

"A shame there's no mud puddle, Barclay," said Rebecca, referencing a horse race at Archer Hall when he'd fallen after they'd finished and chuckling at the memory. She'd really aggravated him that day.

"It is. I'd love to see you covered in mud this time after losing to me." Barclay snickered, that smug expression returning.

Rebecca rolled her eyes. *Time to put him in his place.* She beat him, but it was a tight and exciting race. Rebecca and Barclay were first and second to cross the finish line, even edging out their fathers.

"You two were riding like mad," Lord Spalding said.

"That's the best I've ever seen you perform," Lord Putnam said to Barclay.

Rebecca and Barclay gazed at one another for a second.

"Rebecca drives me to perform better," Barclay said.

*****

Kenneth

Most of the younger participants were engaged in card games while the older set was out early Thursday afternoon. The morning equestrian races, while diverting, left everyone a little cold, so the indoor activities were a nice reprieve from the wind and rain.

Duke Hartwell exploded into the great room. "What is the meaning of this?" he exclaimed, holding up a letter.

The group looked at one another, confusion on their faces.

"I made myself quite clear, Duke Hartwell," replied Lady Jocelyn.

He rushed towards Kenneth. "You!"

Kenneth jumped out of his chair and held his hands up. "Duke Hartwell, please. What is the matter?"

"This is your fault!" he yelled.

"What is my offense?" Kenneth exclaimed. *I do not want to be on the wrong side of a duke.*

"Lady Jocelyn ended our courtship." Duke Hartwell clenched his jaw.

"I'm sorry, but in the end, you may be the better for it," said Kenneth.

Lord Spalding whistled. "Mr. Barclay, she is a lady."

"A lady who's put me in an impossible position. What did you write in that letter?" he asked her.

"I consider that a private communication," answered Lady Jocelyn.

Kenneth scowled.

"She said her affections had been transferred to another due to my so-called neglect," answered Duke Hartwell.

"What makes you believe I'm the other party?" Kenneth asked.

"Prior conversations led me to conclude there was a dalliance between the two of you."

"There was no romantic attachment." Kenneth glanced at Rebecca. She'd already been uneasy over this issue, and this episode couldn't help that.

Rebecca stared back at him, not upset or angry but rather more curious than anything. Calm.

That's a good sign. Kenneth exhaled. *I don't want to lose her over this.*

"Dalliance might be a touch strong," said Lady Jocelyn. "Though I made it plain I was attracted to him since it appeared my attachment to you was no longer returned."

"And I made it equally evident how I absolutely was not," Kenneth retorted.

Lady Jocelyn nodded. "That's true. At that time."

"My affections never wavered," said Duke Hartwell. "I made that abundantly clear upon my arrival."

Lady Jocelyn smoothed her dress. "Obviously, not apparent enough."

Duke Hartwell glared at Kenneth but took a couple of steps backward.

"I also informed you that Lady Jocelyn didn't make it known that she was attached when she first arrived here," Kenneth said to Duke Hartwell in a quieter tone. "I believe every gentleman here would agree."

"That I will vouch for," Lord Spalding put in. "I spoke to Lady Jocelyn myself on the matter the first night, and it was one of the reasons I sent for you, Richard."

"Why did you not say so in your letter?" Duke Hartwell asked him.

"I didn't wish to sway you in the event Lady Jocelyn had temporarily acted in error, was remorseful, and wished to maintain her relationship with you." He grimaced. "It appears that was a mistake."

Duke Hartwell scanned the group and then stalked out of the room.

Lord Spalding sighed. "I'll go after him."

Lady Jocelyn left as well, citing she had the correspondence she'd put off that she must tend to.

Rebecca pulled Kenneth towards the windows. "Do you think Duke Hartwell will sway Lord Spalding away from your agreement if he remains very angry with you?" she asked quietly.

Kenneth's shoulders sagged. "It's a strong possibility." A wave of panic washed over him. "I meant what I said when I told her I made it abundantly clear how I'm not—"

Rebecca patted his arm. "I know. I don't understand why Lady Jocelyn is carrying out the game to this extent. It's obvious Duke Hartwell is besotted with her. I can try to soothe things over between you and him."

"Thank you. I'd greatly appreciate that."

Rebecca led him out into the hallway and kissed his cheek. "You should take a rest. The old governess room has a bed and is available."

Kenneth nodded, feeling drained. He squeezed her hand and wandered slowly down the hall.

How did I get in the middle of such a mess?

*****

Rebecca

Rebecca stepped into the library. "Duke Hartwell!" she exclaimed and then curtsied. "I didn't expect to see anyone in here."

He offered her a peaked smile. "The room is yours. I was about to speak with your father as I'll probably depart shortly."

"I'm sorry for what has occurred."

"I'm not the first man to be tossed aside by a lady, and I won't be the last."

"Is there anything we can do to ease your mind and persuade you to stay? We'll be saddened by your departure, and I'm more inclined to have Lady Jocelyn leave."

Duke Hartwell regarded her for a moment. "You speak as though you don't like her, even though she's your friend."

"I haven't liked some of her behavior during this visit," Rebecca replied carefully. "It may have been unwise to become quickly and closely acquainted."

"You and I both," Duke Hartwell muttered. "And what of Mr. Barclay? How sure are you of his affections?"

"I'm sure of them now. Why do you ask?"

"A woman of your caliber should be treated with more appreciation than he accords you."

Rebecca swallowed. "In his defense, he's known me since I was born and has witnessed firsthand a lot of my silly and childish behavior. Lady Jocelyn's presence here is probably one of the worst examples of such conduct."

Duke Hartwell raised an eyebrow. "How so?"

Rebecca enlightened him on the circumstances of Lady Jocelyn's visit. "My actions and suggestions were calloused and gave little thought to the feelings of others. I never wished to pain you this way and beg your pardon."

He slumped in his chair. "It's not your fault, Miss Tarleton. You were brought into the middle of a courtship that was apparently not sound."

Rebecca shook her head. "I recklessly interfered where I shouldn't. My actions put Mr. Barclay in a difficult position, and he has born it well." Rebecca paused. "And it's intriguing that this transpired after Mr. Udayle's departure, creating distrust between you and your partners, personal and business."

Duke Hartwell appeared to take stock of her. "Indeed, it is."

"It appears he knows you well and how to strike effectively."

"Are you reconsidering your investment, Miss Tarleton?"

She contemplated for a moment how to answer. "Not at present, and like I said before, I'm sure in Barclay, so I'll stand behind him." She hesitated. "But I don't know you as well. The potential for your personal life to interfere with your business decisions is a serious threat and one I'll closely monitor."

"I understand." He pressed his lips together. "I'm still miffed by Mr. Barclay, but that's probably more from jealousy than anything. It does appear that he acted properly and, as you said, has born the situation well." He stood. "I must leave early. My presence has made things unpleasant enough."

Rebecca exhaled after he left the library, wholeheartedly ashamed of herself. *How could I be so thoughtless?*

CHAPTER 24

Changes on the Horizon

Rebecca

"I thank you for your hospitality," Duke Hartwell said to Rebecca as she saw him off later that afternoon.

Papa had tried to talk him into staying but also understood why that would be uncomfortable. Duke Hartwell seemed more embarrassed than anything; there appeared to be no lingering anger towards anyone except Lady Jocelyn. Rebecca hadn't told her of his imminent departure as she believed that news should come from him, or she could receive it after he'd left.

Lady Jocelyn walked into the area. "You're leaving?" she asked Duke Hartwell, perplexed.

"Yes. There's no other reason for me to stay," Duke Hartwell said tightly. "And I have many matters to oversee."

Lady Jocelyn crossed her arms and pouted. "This is certainly evidence that you never cared for me. You act as though it were nothing I had to break off our courtship."

His eyes grew enormous. "Of course, I care for you, Lady Jocelyn."

"You say that, but I don't believe it," she cut in petulantly. "You didn't act the part. I really felt quite abandoned by you."

Rebeca stifled a sound of disgust.

"What would you have me do?" Duke Hartwell cried out.

"You should fight for me if you care so much."

She must be joking.

Duke Hartwell appeared confused. "Fight for you?"

Lady Jocelyn nodded.

"With whom?" he asked. "It doesn't appear any of the other men—"

Lady Jocelyn's eyes blazed.

"Of course, fight for you with you." Duke Hartwell rubbed his forehead. "I suppose I'll remain then."

"I knew you were an excellent nobleman and gentleman, a true duke. In time, I may accept your renewal of our courtship." Beaming, Lady Jocelyn swept upstairs.

Rebecca's jaw dropped. *Is Lady Jocelyn insane? What just happened here?* She gaped at Duke Hartwell. *I can't... what is wrong with this man?* "I truly fear for your emotional well-being right now."

He threw her a sheepish grin. "I hope your offer to stay remains."

"Absolutely, and I'm delighted that you're doing so. However, if you seriously renew your attentions toward Lady Jocelyn, I'll question your ability to reason soundly. And I say that with the utmost respect and care for your person."

He chuckled. "You don't mince words. I understand your reservations, but Lady Jocelyn had a couple of valid points. I've been neglectful."

"Your father died. She could keep as you tend to those matters, and it would be to her benefit for you to do so."

He still looked unsure.

"Given her behavior, she should beg you for her pardon, not the other way around."

"But I do like her a great deal, Miss Tarleton. And we don't have evidence that she colluded with Mr. Udayle; it's sheer conjecture. Would it do any harm to give this another chance?"

"I do hope sincerely that no harm comes, and you're a better judge for your happiness than me."

"I appreciate your concern," he said as he walked back into the house.

Rebecca gave instructions to the housekeeper to return the duke's things to his quarters.

Lord Eamon appeared. "I didn't mean to be so late. What's happening?"

"Duke Hartwell will stay."

"That's good, right?"

"He might regret that decision. He and Lady Jocelyn are to try again."

Papa raised an eyebrow.

"I know," Rebecca said. "But I'm happy he's staying."

"Let's see if we can help him out."

*****

Kenneth

Duke Hartwell entered the great room. "Mr. Barclay!"

Kenneth stilled. He was about to depart for the day. Leaving earlier would look like he was running away, but it was awkward to remain. Kenneth figured he'd ride home and take supper there, and Notley and his father could stay or go with him as they wished.

Duke Hartwell walked towards him. "If you would favor me with a few minutes discourse."

Barclay nodded and followed him to the far side of the room, away from the others.

"After speaking with Spalding and a couple of the other gentlemen, I want to apologize for any discomfort myself or Lady Jocelyn has put you through," Duke Hartwell said quietly. "It appears as though you really were imposed upon."

Kenneth exhaled. "I never meant you any discourtesy or harm—"

Duke Hartwell stuck out his hand. "It's forgotten if you can grant us the same pardon."

Kenneth pumped his hand. "Of course."

"Now, we have a business venture to review."

Ten minutes later, the two men, Spalding, and Rebecca were seated at the massive oak table in the library.

Kenneth gaped at them after Spalding made the duke disclose some of his history with Mr. Udayle.

"With all due respect, Duke Hartwell, I don't want my ships undermined because of a school-age spat between you and Mr. Udayle," Kenneth said.

"I understand, and Miss Tarleton expressed the same concerns. I promise I'll be more transparent about such histories moving forward if they'll impact our operations."

"Thank you," Barclay said to Duke Hartwell.

"Your competition sailing may be an excellent opportunity for us to conduct further business," Duke Hartwell said. "Miss Tarleton, I own an office and showroom for the machinery I promote not far from where Mr. Barclay does his shipbuilding. If you're agreeable, I'll invite you both to my home in London, where we could consider the arrangements and view the equipment. And I'd imagine Spalding will already be there."

He nodded.

"I'd like that," Rebecca answered. "Thank you for the invitation."

They discussed further preparations, and then Duke Hartwell and Spalding left to see Lady Jocelyn.

"It's thrilling to work on a project like this together." He squeezed her hand.

"Just the beginning, I hope."

"Absolutely." He leaned over and kissed her.

"I hate to think how often you two actually engage in that, seeing as every time I run into you, it's happening," Lord Eamon said from the door.

Kenneth cringed. "It's been literally only when you've seen us."

"Kenneth, I'd like a little time with my daughter, if you don't mind."

He jumped up and gave Lord Eamon a hurried bow as he rushed out of the room.

*****

Rebecca

"Papa," Rebecca admonished gently.

Her father was chuckling as he took the seat Barclay had vacated. "I love playing with his thinking faculties."

Rebecca shook her head. "What is it you wish to discuss?"

He sobered. "Your courtship is developing at a rapid rate."

"It's been scarce a week."

"Yet, you and Kenneth read like a married couple. I'm surprised at how quickly that pattern formed."

Rebecca smiled. "It's wonderful."

"It is." He paused. "Make sure you know, Rebecca."

She studied her father. "You doubt Barclay?"

"Fundamentally no, but make certain he's grown as he should, and more importantly, that you feel secure in him. Are you unsure of my care and love for you?"

"Never. There's nothing I'm more convinced of."

"You should feel the same with Kenneth. Even more so."

As much as she cared for Barclay, she wasn't there yet.

"Give things the proper time," Papa said. "And it relieves my mind to know that if events follow to their natural conclusion, you'll be in the family of one of my closest friends and well-loved. I'm very pleased."

Rebecca beamed.

"I should've had this talk with you long before now," Lord Eamon said. "I didn't want to face the fact that you'll leave me at some point."

Rebecca linked arms with him. "It's not like I haven't courted, Papa."

"It's never been this serious." He exhaled. "If you give birth to a son, Stoddard Grove will go to him. Otherwise, it'll most likely pass to Repington."

Rebecca regarded her father. "You don't expect to remarry?"

He was quiet for a moment. "The older I get, the less likely it'll be that I'll have a male heir."

"True, but I doubt you're at that point yet."

"You sound like Percival. I've never been in a hurry to marry again, but perhaps my feelings on that will change once you are. At least with Laidley Park, you'll still be nearby until it's time for Kenneth to take his place at Archer Hall."

"Hopefully, not anytime soon," Rebecca said softly.

"Yes, I desire that as well. I believe everyone is happier with the current state and arrangement of things. I'll also make adjustments to your dowry," Papa continued. "I kept it modest because I wasn't certain what attention you'd attract. But with Kenneth and the Barclays, I'll be more generous, and I want to be assured you're cared for should anything happen to all of us."

"Thank you, Papa, that's most kind."

"I am very proud of you, beloved daughter. Now go find your love lost suitor and do whatever it is the two of you do."

Rebecca kissed her father goodbye and ran from the room.

CHAPTER 25

Clouded Vision

Rebecca

The last event was 'fish as you wish' on Friday and Saturday, with extra points awarded for the largest catch. Rebecca's father would announce the final standings and the winners at the closing celebration meal on Sunday before their guests left.

Fishing wasn't Rebecca's favorite activity, and she didn't intend to be an active participant. But it was growing difficult for her to spend time with Lady Jocelyn, and doing so in a larger group would make the task easier. She hoped they could keep their friendship if Lady Jocelyn regained her senses, but Rebecca needed to retain her sanity in the meantime. Fortunately, Duke Hartwell was attentive, so Lady Jocelyn was occupied.

The company split into fours, and Rebecca was with Lady Jocelyn, Duke Hartwell, and Barclay. Their fathers' foursome was within sight. The day was overcast, but it was warmer than usual and not windy.

Maybe we'll get through this with no problems.

Duke Hartwell gave a contented exhalation. "I always pictured myself doing this with a couple of sons."

"You must enjoy fishing a great deal," commented Barclay.

"I do. I'm searching for the perfect spot. This is pleasant, but I'd choose something more picturesque."

"You don't find fishing dreadfully dull?" Lady Jocelyn asked, perched on a nearby rock.

"I prefer the term relaxing," Duke Hartwell said. "One can meditate and meld with nature."

"We've done a great deal of melding with nature the last couple of weeks," Lady Jocelyn said dryly.

"It sounds marvelous," said Duke Hartwell. "I wish I could've been here the whole time."

"I'll inform my father," said Rebecca. "He'd be pleased and honored to invite you for future hunts."

"Thank you. I'd enjoy that," Duke Hartwell replied. "I can see why Spalding is such an enthusiast of his. I thought at first you might have been my friend's objective, Miss Tarleton."

Rebecca flushed. "No indeed. I feel Lord Spalding is more grown than I. I'm sure he had no such thoughts."

"Where does that put me?" Barclay asked.

Rebecca smirked. "We're on the same page, Barclay."

Lady Jocelyn sighed loudly. "Hartwell, can't you spend time with me instead of the boring fish? Why don't we take a walk?"

A frown flashed across his face before it transformed into a bright smile aimed at Lady Jocelyn. "Of course. I'll come back to this later."

The two walked off.

"I wonder how that courtship will proceed the second go-round," Barclay said. "I feel bad for Duke Hartwell, but I like having you to myself for a bit."

"This is nice, and he agreed to court her again, so my pity is in small supply."

Barclay chuckled, and they stood quietly on the bank for a while.

"Do you desire to have children?" Barclay asked.

"Why do you ask?"

It seemed an odd query, though the duke had mentioned sons, so she supposed it wasn't out of the blue. Even if she didn't wish for children, there weren't many options. Women were expected to have babies, especially to carry on the family name, title, and estate. Rebecca didn't personally take issue with that entrustment, but it was vexing that in the minds of a few, this was a mandate and the sole reason women walked the earth. She had a sneaking suspicion Barclay wouldn't have asked that question of any other lady he'd court, and that upset her more.

"You've never mentioned having children," he replied.

"We've only lately been in a relationship where we'd have such a discussion."

"So you don't?"

"I do. Why would you assume I wouldn't?"

He shrugged. "You're near the top of the leaderboard in this hunt."

"What does that have to do with anything?" she asked sharply.

"I'm not acquainted with any mothers who shoot like you."

"I fail to see why the two are mutually exclusive."

"It doesn't have to be. You hardly seem the motherly type."

Rebecca recoiled. *How is it that Lady Jocelyn can treat and use men so severely, and they fall all over themselves for her, and I act like myself and try to treat everyone well, yet I'm deemed not motherly or ladylike enough?* "You keep reminding me how I'm no lady," she snapped.

"I said you were refined enough," he shot back.

"Refined enough," she muttered. "That's a ringing endorsement for femininity."

"Since when did you want to be so-called feminine? Where is this coming from?" Barclay exclaimed. "You're fine."

"Just not a mother for your children," she retorted.

"Obviously, I don't feel that way since I'm courting you! Why are you constantly yelling at me?"

"Why are you constantly blind? You don't understand anything!"

*****

Kenneth

I might not understand certain things, but I know Rebecca. "Perhaps my vision is fine, and you don't like what I'm seeing," he said coldly.

Rebecca paled. "You always discern how to destroy me, don't you?" She stalked off.

"Rebecca!" Kenneth ran after her.

"And I keep letting you."

"Getting torn down by you all the time hasn't been a picnic either."

"Then why are we courting?" She whirled on him. "Clearly, we make each other miserable."

"And now you expect me, the man who sees nothing and never acts, to do something about it?" he taunted.

"We're done!"

"Quitting like the child you are. No wonder you never spoke of having a family."

She screamed again and rushed him.

Rebecca

Rebecca was suddenly jerked backward. Her father said her name in a very firm but calm voice as he dragged her away.

When did he get here? She stopped flailing and glanced back at Barclay.

His eyes were hard.

"What has gotten into you?" Papa asked once they were some distance away.

"I despise him!" She yelled as she broke out of her father's hold and started pacing. She let out another scream, but it came out like a strangled cry. "I loathe him because he's right."

"Perhaps you ought to take a ride or a walk." Papa's voice was still low, but it sounded alarmed.

Rebecca didn't blame him. She was frightening herself. This situation was eerily reminiscent of when he'd found her in the forest all those years ago. Rebecca had been so terrified, she'd almost beaten him with a tree limb until realizing it was him.

I'm still lost. I can't see my way out of this.

"The two of you can patch things up later," he said.

"No. We're done. Because I can't be what he wants." Rebecca swallowed the lump in her throat.

"He wants you. This doesn't make sense."

No, he doesn't. I'm not enough. I can't conquer this. Rebecca walked past her father. "I'll be back."

CHAPTER 26

Frozen

Kenneth

Kenneth swallowed as Lord Eamon made his way towards him.

"I haven't seen her that upset since the day I found her in the woods," Rebecca's father said. "What happened?"

"I don't know. I don't understand."

"She said you two were finished. Is that true?"

"Rebecca has the right to end a courtship unilaterally, but I'm fighting for us first."

Lord Eamon nodded as though pleased with that answer. "What did you say to her?"

"I only asked if she wanted children."

Lord Eamon appeared amused. "Why would you ask her that?"

"I was curious, so I inquired. I thought nothing of it."

"And if she'd said no?"

Kenneth shrugged. "Then I know she doesn't."

"You wouldn't consider ending the courtship?"

"Of course not. I suppose it was a careless way of forming an idea of what kind of family size I could envision. I need an heir, but there's a tremendous difference between one child and a cricket team."

"How are you planning on controlling that?"

"I don't know! I'm an idiot. I merely wanted to see how Rebecca felt."

"And that was all you said?"

"That and she didn't seem the motherly type."

Lord Eamon gave him a look.

"I meant nothing by that! Is Rebecca like any mother you've met?" Kenneth asked him desperately. "None of the mothers I'm acquainted with can shoot enough game to feed their family, outride any man, then be a wonderful hostess for a dinner party at her home. And somewhere amid all that, speak Mongolian and help construct a catapult. Where did she come from? She's not like any man of my experience. She's Rebecca, this beautiful, wondrous being all her own—"

"And I take it, you explained none of this to her?" Lord Eamon asked wryly.

"I was too angry at that point and said a couple of things that were probably true but shouldn't have been expressed in the manner I did, and then she tried to attack me."

Lord Eamon shook his head and chuckled. "Kenneth, you can't seem to get out of your own way, can you?"

The two stood in silence.

"It pleases me you care about her opinion on matters like childbearing," said Lord Eamon. "That's taken for granted."

"I care about her. Why is Rebecca so unhappy with herself?" Kenneth asked quietly.

I may be blind to some points, but that's shockingly clear to me. It concerned him more than anything, and his harsh words once again did nothing to alleviate that. *How do I fix it? What should I do to make her happy?*

"I don't understand it myself." Lord Eamon sat heavily on a nearby rock. "She and I were two peas in a pod for so long. It was like after she got out in society, she slowly became unsure of herself. I tried to do right by her—"

"You're a good father."

"Perhaps I should have remarried and given her a mother—"

"But she's fine. Rebecca is fine the way she is."

"Absolutely. Please don't cease reminding her of that."

Kenneth grabbed his bag and pole. "I'll find her now and remind her again."

"Secure her, son, as she does you."

Kenneth nodded and walked off.

*****

Rebecca

Are we done? Did I really do that?

It was ironic the place Rebecca retreated to was the woods. But somehow, it gave her solace, like she had made peace with it. Even if Rebecca couldn't completely control everything here, she could work with it. She was no longer helpless.

But Kenneth's words made her feel helpless.

He went from not seeing me at all to seeing me too clearly.

Maybe he's always seen me.

Or according to him, I'm the one who doesn't like the image. But I knew that. What does he see?

Why can't I see it anymore?

Rebecca stopped her horse. She didn't catch sight of stag frequently, and he was an especially large one with an impressive set of antlers.

Rebecca smiled. *He's a handsome fellow.*

Her father said it was best to leave them alone this time of year, as they could be much more aggressive. She watched the stag for a few moments from afar and then spied a couple of female deer sipping water from the tiny stream nearby. A beautiful scene, but best to go. She was about to ride quietly away when she saw Barclay.

Interesting, he'd retreat here as well.

But he's much too close. He probably doesn't realize the stag is there. Barclay was on foot, right between the female and the stag.

Where is his horse?

The stag rose on its hind legs and started charging, head bent with that impressive set of antlers frontward.

"Kenneth!" Rebecca screamed and charged Mason. Barclay froze.

I'm so sorry, beautiful stag. With a strength Rebecca didn't know she possessed, she whipped out her pistol. She'd never done this riding Mason at full tilt.

Bang!

Mason reared up on his hindquarters. Rebecca was so fixated on the stag she didn't retain control. She got off one more shot before she fell through the air.

And then blackness engulfed her.

*****

Kenneth

I'm going to die.

Kenneth hit the ground, tasting dirt, when he'd heard the bangs.

Rebecca.

He shot up from the soil, the stag on its side about 20 yards away, alive but incapacitated.

Rebecca lay in a crumpled heap on the grass near her horse, which was jumping around.

Kenneth ran over, his heart in his throat as he felt for her pulse. Faint but there. The ground was softer and mossier here; that might have cushioned her fall.

Unusually skittish, Rebecca's horse neighed as he walked back and forth in jerky motions. Kenneth calmed him down. *I don't blame you, chap. I feel the same way.*

I froze, and I hurt Rebecca because of it. Kenneth was paralyzed, not knowing how to get her back to the house safely.

'I've been waiting so long for you to become a man of action.' His father's words played through his head.

I failed.

"Kenneth," Rebecca mumbled.

He was on his knees beside her in a flash. "I'm here."

Think. Act. Kenneth inhaled and slowly surveyed his surroundings, feeling calmer. They weren't along the edge of the forest, so it would take time to travel to Stoddard Grove to fetch help, and getting a conveyance here wouldn't be easy. Kenneth was also troubled leaving her with such a faint pulse.

"I'll get you back," he whispered.

Kenneth examined Rebecca's situation and condition. He didn't think he could transport her on their horses, who were already uneasy. That left carrying her. *Cradle her like a baby or carry her on my back?* Emotionally, he wanted to cradle Rebecca like a baby, but rationally piggyback was the best way to use all his strength, though that felt barbaric.

Kenneth knelt behind her and started to reposition her gently. *She's so small and light.* He'd never thought of her as being so. Rebecca's presence of being was so large it seemed to overtake her actual stature.

After he carefully maneuvered her on his back, he looked for their horses, hoping they'd follow.

Rebecca's horse was right beside him, with his close behind.

CHAPTER 27

What Do You See?

Kenneth

Several hours later, Kenneth was leaning against a wall outside of Rebecca's rooms. His father and Lord Eamon walked into the corridor, and Kenneth leaped off the wall. "How is she?"

Rebecca's father clapped his shoulder. "The doctor said she should be fine. We need to watch her, and she requires rest and quiet right now."

Kenneth exhaled.

"Go in to her," Lord Eamon said. "She's been anxious for you."

Kenneth gave a half-hysterical laugh. "Anxious for me? She was the one who appeared dead on the ground."

Lord Eamon cringed. "I can imagine how horrible that image was. But her last sight was a two hundred pound stag charging you. She had no idea if you were dead or alive."

"Alive thanks to her, and she almost died because of me."

"How so?" Lord Putnam asked.

"I froze," Kenneth replied. "I couldn't act when I had to."

"Most people would have that response in those circumstances," his father said. "Rebecca was extraordinary, acting with the presence of mind she did."

"I don't deserve her."

"Take heart." Lord Eamon said. "You have more going than you give yourself credit for. You did carry her a half-mile."

Kenneth walked into her room quietly as the doctor gathered his things.

Rebecca appeared fragile in the bed, clothed in a white dressing gown and enveloped by blankets. Deep red curls surrounded her head like a crown, making a sharp contrast to the white of the linens.

She held out her hand. "I'm so happy to see you."

He sat next to her bed and kissed her palm.

"I was so scared when that stag stood on its hind legs. I can't imagine losing you."

He rubbed her knuckles. "Try not to think about it. I'm fine."

She studied him. "You don't sound it, and you look sad."

Kenneth mustered up a smile. "I'm sorry. I'm relieved you're doing better."

"Now I can sleep easy. I'm suddenly exhausted."

He kissed her cheek. "Then rest, and I'll visit you in the morning."

Kenneth was surprised both their fathers were still in the corridor.

Lord Eamon threw an arm around his shoulder. "Walk with us for a bit."

The three men went outside. The hour was marching on, and they would need to go home shortly for supper.

"You're still trapped in the past, Kenneth," his father said quietly.

"I don't see Rebecca the same way."

"But you haven't changed how you view yourself," Father replied.

Kenneth stopped short.

"See what Rebecca sees," Lord Eamon said.

"I don't comprehend what that is," Kenneth responded. *Why on earth does she bother with me? How do I secure someone when I'm a disaster myself?*

Lord Eamon grinned. "You should ask her."

*****

The next day, Rebecca looked at Kenneth, confused. "I don't understand. I did hit my head pretty hard yesterday."

Kenneth winced. "We don't have to discuss this now."

"You simply want to hear how I'd describe you?"

He nodded.

"You're tall with light brown hair and brown eyes and—"

"I meant me as a person. It's a wonder you consider me at all," Kenneth said quietly, echoing Lady Jocelyn's words earlier in the week.

Rebecca pondered him. "Are you unsure of my affection?" She swallowed. "Of course, you are. I ended our courtship after that horrible row we had—"

"I informed your father we're going to fight on that."

A smile played on her lips. "Did you?"

Kenneth nodded. "My question was more why you like me. As far as I can see, I'm a whimpering, spineless man who sits on his hands and has treated you with disrespect."

"Kenneth," she said softly.

"Is it not true?"

She smiled. "You're the only person I'm acquainted with who has somehow simultaneously achieved being incredibly earnest with hesitancy. I don't know how you do it."

Kenneth snorted. "I'm very talented."

She closed her eyes. "You try; things go wrong, and you make mistakes, so you try again. Occasionally, you shrink back, but you attempt to correct matters and keep going."

Kenneth thought about her words. "That sounds like me and the right mess that I am."

Rebecca patted his hand. "You're still figuring it out, but you don't suppress that fact. You leave your actions and person in the open for everyone to view." She bit her lip. "The rest of us try to cover ourselves, like a masquerade of sorts."

"You're wonderful the way you are, with nothing to hide," Kenneth said forcefully. "You believe that?"

"The knowledge is there, but I have to convince myself again."

"That's what I'm here for, and I'll work harder at treating you with more consideration in public and private."

"And you wonder why I like you. You didn't slink away when I tried to push you off. Instead, you called me a quitter, held your ground, and told my father you were fighting for us. I love you for all of that, and in my turn, I'll try to treat you with more respect in company and in private." She cupped his cheek. "Now, why do you care for me?"

He grinned. "You're very nice to look at."

She hit his arm. "I poured my heart out to you, and you're telling me that?"

He chuckled and then grew serious. "You impart

confidence and make me act. I know who I am when I'm with you, and I'm comfortable with it. And I love you for that." Kenneth stood. "I'll let you rest."

Rebecca laid back down. "Yes, that was quite a heavy conversation, and I do feel drained."

"I won't bother you the rest of the day."

Rebecca pouted. "You can bother me a little."

Kenneth smiled. "Do you think you'll be strong enough for the big dinner tomorrow?"

"I hope so. I'm tired and achy but not too awful."

Feeling like he was on a firm footing, Kenneth left invigorated.

CHAPTER 28

Hovering

Rebecca

Rebecca opened her eyes the next day, momentarily disoriented. Usually, her room was bathed in light during the morning, even when overcast, but it was dark today. Her curtains were shut tight, and the only illumination came from the fire in the fireplace.

She slowly smiled as her conversation with Barclay the previous afternoon trickled into her thoughts.

We're not done. We're better than ever. That memory swaddled Rebecca in warmth and comfort, even though her muscles still ached.

Papa poked his head into her room. "You're awake. Would you like dinner brought up to you?"

"Dinner?" Rebecca asked. "What about breakfast?"

He gently sat on the edge of her bed. "We had that about five hours ago. The celebration feast will be in another hour."

Rebecca gasped. "I want to be there."

"Are you sure you're up for it?"

"I'm tired, but I wish to be with everyone," she insisted. "I may need additional assistance dressing."

Her father had two maids help her into a simple dress and one of her more ornate robes with velvet along the edges. She left her hair out since her head was tender.

Rebecca tentatively walked downstairs with a girl assisting her. But she was happy to be mobile and eager to see everyone for the conclusion of the festivities.

Rebecca halted on the staircase. Lady Jocelyn was in extremely close proximity to Barclay and then leaped back. Or Barclay pushed her back.

It was a very odd scene.

"Miss Tarleton, I'm sorry you witnessed that," Lady Jocelyn said breathlessly.

"I told you he needs to pay you better regard," Duke Hartwell said tightly behind her.

Rebecca jumped and turned. So this was the object.

"Barclay holds me in esteem," replied Rebecca. "And I'd commented you could find a better partner."

Lady Jocelyn glared at her.

Rebecca shot her a challenging look back.

"Lady Jocelyn, I never want to see you again," Duke Hartwell said.

"But darling—" she began.

"Enough," he snapped.

"I should have chosen Mr. Udayle." Lady Jocelyn sneered. "He was far more entertaining. Actually had some backbone."

"Better alone than with a lady like you. Or possibly any woman, for that matter." Duke Hartwell stormed off.

Lady Jocelyn huffed and ran up the stairs.

Barclay took Rebecca's arm so the maid could leave. "I wager that'll be all over the house in five minutes flat."

Rebecca leaned against him. "What did she do now?"

"She performed a falling into me theatric. I was so astonished. I don't perceive her aim," Barclay commented as they slowly walked towards the great room. "This is hardly an effective way to find a husband."

Rebecca reflected on that. "I rather wonder if she really wants one. At least now."

"Do you believe she's amusing herself? She did ask if I was doing the same with you."

Rebecca thought about Lady Jocelyn. "I think she craves attention and affection but is hesitant to give it back. She was horribly taken advantage of in her first courtship."

"I feel bad for that, but Duke Hartwell seems a decent man."

"It wasn't an excuse, only a vague explanation for her behavior. It appears Lady Jocelyn isn't dealing well with her demons, and something tells me Mr. Udayle won't be the answer either."

"Do you want to help her try?"

Rebecca considered that. "I'd like to, but she can't hurt those I care for in the process."

Rebecca's attention was arrested as she beheld the great room, for this far exceeded her imagination. Father and the servants outdid themselves. She was sorry she missed the setup, for it must have been gratifying to put this together.

All the inserts had been placed into the table, so it was now extra long. It was draped with a lovely plum-colored tablecloth and had a beautiful centerpiece with a woodsy appearance, complete with red candles, acorns, pine combs, and other decorative things. The sideboards and table were overflowing with food and beverages, and the fire was going strong. Papa had gifts for the winners and all the participants on a smaller stand in the corner. He'd even hired a pianist, so there'd be music tonight.

Rebecca was glad she'd made an effort to come down.

Barclay helped her into an oversized upholstered chair close to the fireplace and knelt beside her. "Can I get you anything? Something to drink?"

Rebecca nodded, and Barclay took off.

She leaned back. Even that bit of exertion was exhausting.

Mr. Fitzpatrick pulled a chair alongside her. "We weren't certain if we'd be able to say goodbye. How are you recovering?"

"I need help to do even the simplest of tasks, but I'm strong enough to be present, so I'm doing well."

"Indeed," Mr. Fitzpatrick replied. "With the aid of Barclay's description, a small contingent of us found the spot. The stag was still there, dead, of course. Those were skilled shots, Miss Tarleton. You most likely saved Barclay's life."

Rebecca flushed. "I'm relieved and delighted he's all right, but sad I had to kill the stag. He was lovely."

"He was a magnificent creature. Your father hopes it'll provide excellent meat. Certainly, Mr. Barclay will see to you, but if you need anything tonight, please let me know, and I'd be happy to assist," Mr. Fitzpatrick offered.

"Thank you. You're most kind."

He walked away towards Mr. Baxter, who'd entered the room.

Rebecca watched Mr. Fitzpatrick. *He's rather the mystery man. I wonder what he'll do with himself.*

Barclay returned with a drink and a small plate of bread and jam. He grabbed a blanket and pulled a footrest under her feet. After tucking the covering around her, he took the seat Mr. Fitzpatrick had just vacated.

Rebecca sipped her punch. "You don't have to hover over me, Barclay. I'll probably be quiet tonight watching everyone."

"It's fine. I can sit with you."

Lord Spalding and Repington walked in. Repington said something to the Fitzpatrick brothers and Mr. Baxter, and then the four roared with laughter.

Rebecca patted Barclay's leg. "Go visit with the other gentlemen. I know you enjoy being with them."

"You're positive you're okay?" he asked her.

"Stop fussing over me!" She gave him a playful shove.

Barclay grinned and joined the others.

Rebecca shook her head as she leaned back again and relaxed. *He's a mess. But he's mine.*

*****

Kenneth

Moments of clarity regarding Rebecca seemed to come in lightning strikes to Kenneth. He glanced at her as he crossed the room to join the other gentlemen.

"I'm surprised you could tear yourself away, Barclay," said Spalding.

"She made me leave her," Kenneth replied. "Accused me of hovering."

"And you said it would never happen," Repington teased.

"I'm glad I was wrong."

"I have to say your methods were truly unusual," Spalding said. "Most entertaining, but definitely odd."

"Probably because I didn't employ any methods," Kenneth remarked. "Unfortunately for Miss Tarleton, she got the rough, unpolished Barclay. I was quite myself."

"Perhaps that was best then," said Mr. Baxter.

"I plan on making up for it. I'm going to smother her with attention and affection."

"Which is why she sent you away," joked Repington.

"I might need to give her some space to breathe," Kenneth said. "I rarely get this stuff right the first time."

Notley entered the room with Duke Hartwell, who still appeared stormy.

"Hartwell!" Spalding called. "What ails you?"

"Lady Jocelyn," he grumbled.

The men exchanged looks.

"What happened now?"

"We're done," he ground out. "That woman is a charlatan, a snake to play with men's affections for her own amusement—"

Spalding clapped his shoulder. "Let's try not to think about her."

Duke Hartwell grunted. "I've learned my lesson. No women."

Repington snorted.

"You don't believe I can do it?" Duke Hartwell asked. "Don't need them. I'm married to my pursuits."

Spalding did not seem convinced.

"I'm serious," Duke Hartwell insisted.

"I'm sure you are," said Spalding dryly. "I'll check with you in a month's time. What happened to working on an heir?"

Duke Hartwell crossed his arms. "I just won't die."

The others snickered.

Lord Eamon made his entrance, and the young men yelled for him. They said their thanks and words of appreciation before he excused himself to see after Rebecca.

"It's a wonder he never remarried," commented Notley.

"He's a smart man."

"Hartwell," Spalding chided.

"He did fine on his own," Duke Hartwell insisted. "Consider how well Miss Tarleton turned out. He didn't need a woman."

"Perhaps some food will make you less ill-humored." Spalding dragged him towards the sideboard.

"How determined do you think he is?" Baxter asked Fitzpatrick.

"I'm not sure," he replied thoughtfully. "Generally, Hartwell is affable. But he can be single-minded if he wishes, and experiencing disappointment in a relationship could certainly put him there."

Lady Jocelyn surveyed the room from the doorway. Mr. Adams walked in behind her and said a few words, and they strolled towards the window on the far side.

Notley nudged Mr. Baxter. "We're in the best position to make this less uncomfortable."

They joined Lady Jocelyn and Mr. Adams.

Fitzpatrick smiled at Kenneth. "If you like, we can hover over Miss Tarleton."

Kenneth grinned. "Grand idea."

CHAPTER 29

Hunt Celebration Dinner

Kenneth

A little while later, Lord Eamon called the group to attention. "First, I'll announce the standings, and then we'll eat."

The company eagerly took their seats around the table. Rebecca and her father were at opposite ends of the table. They'd moved the immense chair she'd been in so she could still rest. Kenneth sat in his chair in the center. That seemed to be his place during this event, in the middle of things.

I suppose I have an identity now.

Kenneth had been so determined to win in the beginning, and now he hardly cared. The time here was better than winning. The opposing team won, though his group had pulled out a strong showing during the second half, so it had turned into a close contest. Lord Eamon had fine silver mugs for each member of the winning team with the event and date engraved on them. Many of them used their prize to help themselves to rum.

Fitzpatrick came in third. Rebecca had edged him out for second place.

Kenneth's father won the grand prize. He admired the bow Lord Eamon handed him. "This is a fine piece of craftsmanship, Gregory. Thank you."

"I suppose my daughter will be a passenger on your boat, Kenneth." Lord Eamon chuckled.

"Gladly," Kenneth replied. "She can handle all the pirates that board."

"You'll have to find another companion, Miss Tarleton," Lady Jocelyn said coolly. "Such a voyage wouldn't be good for my constitution."

Rebecca seemed to breathe a sigh of relief. "I'd be happy to recruit a replacement."

"That wouldn't be necessary if you married me," said Kenneth.

Rebecca laughed softly. "I thought you wished to wrap this project up soon."

"I do. And I'm serious," Kenneth said.

Rebecca's eyes widened. "What?"

"Will you marry me?" asked Kenneth. "Please."

She blinked at him. "I'll have to say no to that."

Kenneth felt a stab. "Of course. I understand."

"I'm not sure that you do," Rebecca said. "I want to be with you."

"But you don't want to marry me."

"Not yet. Barclay, we courted for a week and argued for half of it."

Repington chuckled.

"Doesn't one usually ask those sorts of things in private?" Spalding asked, sounding mildly amused.

"Generally," agreed Kenneth's father wryly.

"But we've known each other forever, and we always argue." Kenneth was focused solely on Rebecca.

"Kenneth." She rubbed her temples.

"Please continue to be patient with my son," his father said. "He's getting used to this man of action thing."

Lord Eamon chortled.

"Father." Kenneth glared at him.

"There's taking action, and then there's moving too quickly," he replied.

Kenneth looked at Rebecca.

She nodded. "Let's slow our pace and be sure."

"But I'm certain."

"How?"

"Sometimes you know."

Rebecca gifted him with a slow, beautiful smile. "I understand," she said gently. "But let's enjoy courting for a bit."

Kenneth grinned back. "Yes, and then you'll agree to marry me."

Rebecca gave a hearty laugh. "Then I'll agree to marry you."

The men cheered.

"And if you could ask me privately first, next time—" Rebecca started.

"Right," Kenneth agreed. "Sure thing."

CHAPTER 30

A Flash

Rebecca

Rebecca walked Lady Jocelyn to the entrance-way Monday morning.

"Well, my friend, this was an adventure," said Lady Jocelyn. "Thank you for inviting me."

Rebecca forced a smile. "I'm happy you enjoyed yourself."

"I think I'll continue my correspondence with Mr. Udayle. He was very entertaining," said Lady Jocelyn. "And he'd be interested in all that transpired here."

"What do you mean?" Rebecca asked evenly.

"I'm sure he'd be pleased to hear I'm no longer with Duke Hartwell." She gave Rebecca a smirk. "Whatever did you mean, dear?"

Rebecca narrowed her eyes. *Don't dear me.* She yanked the carriage door wide open. "I wish you a safe journey."

The footman gave her a curious glance and then stepped back.

"Thank you." Lady Jocelyn hopped inside. "I'm sure we'll see one another again soon."

The two women exchanged looks. Something flashed through Lady Jocelyn's eyes.

Fear.

As quickly as it came, the flash was gone, and the cool demeanor Lady Jocelyn usually wore settled back in.

"Goodbye," Rebecca said gently. "Write to inform me you've arrived safely."

"I will," Lady Jocelyn said earnestly. No false manners. No pretenses. No games.

Rebecca shut the door, and the carriage jerked off.

Barclay walked down the steps and stood close behind her. "Is she gone?"

"Yes. She said she would continue corresponding with Mr. Udayle."

"They might be perfect for one another."

"Guard your shipbuilding closely." Rebecca wanted to support Lady Jocelyn, but there was no telling what she and Mr. Udayle could do if they put their heads together.

"Of course. I won't let you down."

"You're not what concerns me. It's outside forces." She reached up and rubbed his cheek. "I don't want you hurt in the crossfire. You were amidst it during your stay."

"The crossfire put me in direct line for you, so we're good. It was all worth it." He leaned down and kissed her.

"Seriously," Lord Eamon said. "Are you trying to make me ill?"

Rebecca giggled. *It must be a special father-daughter sense.*

Barclay groaned. "It isn't as frequent—"

"Aye, I know." Lord Eamon waved a hand. "I don't really care. I just enjoy playing with your brain."

Barclay scowled at him.

Lord Spalding and Mr. Fitzpatrick joined them.

"We'll see you in the spring," Lord Spalding said.

Barclay shook his hand. "Looking forward to it."

Lord Spalding decided it'd be best to test then, and he'd line up the first shipment for around that time, having confidence the vessel would pass with flying colors and that maybe Bonaparte would stop his continental march. The brothers said their goodbyes and departed. The local guests had left yesterday after the celebration dinner, and Duke Hartwell had pulled out earlier that morning. Barclay's father and Notley would leave tomorrow.

"Another hunt over successfully," Barclay said to her father. "How did you enjoy yourself?"

Lord Eamon chuckled. "It was certainly the most eventful one ever. Is that your influence, Kenneth? You show up in the neighborhood, and suddenly, all kinds of things happen."

Rebecca wrapped her arms around Barclay. "I told him he'd create a stir."

CHAPTER 31

A Year of Change

Kenneth

six months later

Kenneth was putting the finishing touches on his wedding apparel. It was astonishing how much had changed over a year. A year ago to almost the week, the Tarletons had visited his family at Archer Hall. Kenneth was utterly infatuated with another, and Rebecca drove him insane.

Now she was driving him insane in a completely different way, and he couldn't wait to wed her.

The butler entered his room. "Lord Vaughnryd asked if you would be so gracious as to grant him a brief interview."

Kenneth stilled. "I'll meet with him."

Even though Rebecca and Hannah were close companions, Kenneth hadn't spoken to Lord Vaughnryd since the day he visited Hannah at Corwyn, and she'd definitively finished any hope of a relationship between them. Lord Vaughnryd and Hannah had married in April. Kenneth had attended the wedding with Rebecca and her father and gave Hannah his warmest wishes.

But otherwise, he'd remained on the periphery and hadn't spoken with Lord Vaughnryd at all.

Kenneth entered the drawing room, and Lord Vaughnryd rose from his chair with a tentative but friendly countenance. "I thank you for seeing me right now. I know you have much to do."

"You're welcome," Kenneth said, relaxing when he realized Lord Vaughnryd was as awkward as he. "How can I help you? It must be important for you to seek me out."

"It's imperative I lay to rest any ill feelings that may be between us. I personally wanted to deliver my congratulations and best wishes to you and Miss Tarleton for a happy marriage."

"Thank you. I bear you no ill will. I didn't want to mar your wedding day."

"I had the same concerns today." Lord Vaughnryd held out his hand. "A new beginning?"

Kenneth shook it firmly. "A new beginning."

"I'll leave you to finish." Lord Vaughnryd began crossing the room and then stopped. "I hear we're to be business associates."

"I must pass inspection first, but if all goes well, we will be."

They sail in a little over a month to test the ship. Kenneth had convinced Rebecca this would not be their wedding trip, arguing he wanted a real trip to celebrate their marriage. They compromised by planning a sea-bathing stay at Weymouth immediately after their marriage until the test voyage.

"There are more improvements underway at Lord Thurston's mill operations," said Lord Vaughnryd. "I have a feeling our eccentric duke will try to talk me into starting another quarry. He has many plans for an abundance of coal, including your ships."

"I told him I wasn't ready for steam yet." Kenneth shook his head. "Nevermind. I'll begin researching and building, as I'm not sure what I agreed to."

"It'll be an adventure, whatever it is." Lord Vaughnryd took his leave.

A year of change indeed.

And now for the biggest change of all. It was time to go to Stoddard Grove and begin his new life with Rebecca.

Epilogue

nine years later

Rebecca

"Clarine, don't forget your archery lesson in thirty minutes," Rebecca reminded her eight-year-old daughter as she entered the morning room at Laidley Park.

She sighed, lifting her pretty fawn-colored eyes from the bonnet she was fixing a ribbon to. "Must I? Why do I need to learn to shoot? Reeves likes those things, and he's a boy."

Rebecca exhaled. They had this argument every time her lesson came around. *How did I get such a girly daughter?* "Archery is a popular courting activity."

It wasn't why Rebecca wanted her to have the lessons, but she figured the argument might quiet her child.

Clarine perked up. "Truly?"

Rebecca nodded.

Clarine set her hat aside. "I'll prepare myself."

Rebecca shook her head as she watched her daughter walk out of the room. *She's eight, turning eighteen, and much too young to have such an interest in those things.*

Footsteps pounded down the hall. "Where's Papa?" her son, Reeves, asked from the doorway.

"In his study," replied Rebecca. "What do you need?"

"A different knife to finish my raft."

"It might be better to discuss such things with your grandfather," Rebecca said. "We can call on him in a bit if you like."

"I'll ask Papa anyway." He took off. Reeves resembled Kenneth's father with piercing gray eyes and dark hair.

Always welcoming amusement, Rebecca followed him to Kenneth's study.

"Papa, I need a special knife," Reeves said.

Kenneth jerked his head up from his papers. "Why?"

Rebecca smothered a laugh.

"My raft," their son answered. "I can't cut the sticks the way I want."

Kenneth relaxed but now seemed confused. "It's a knife. They all cut things."

Reeves gawked at his father. "Papa, different knives do different jobs—"

"Reeves," Rebecca said behind him. "We'll call on your grandfather as soon as I know Clarine is settled with her archery lesson."

He took off down the hall again.

"He's only eight. Why can't I follow what he's speaking of half the time?" Kenneth asked.

Rebecca chuckled. She had been pregnant with Clarine right after Reeves was born, so they're the same age for a short period every year.

"I realize various knives do different jobs, but why does he require it?" Kenneth exhaled. "Isn't he too young to play with knives?"

"I'll take him to Papa. Clarine should be settled with her archery lesson shortly, and then her governess will have studies for her."

"At least we have one child who's civilized."

"Too civilized." She rather enjoyed Reeves's rough and tumble ways. He played the way she believed a little boy should — curious, without fear, and all heart.

"Clarine is wonderful." Kenneth beamed.

Rebecca shook her head. *Clarine is Papa's little princess.* Rebecca crossed the room and kissed Kenneth. "I'll see you later today."

He pulled her onto his lap and kissed her again. "You could stay in here."

She giggled and kissed him thrice. His kisses never grew old. "You heard me promise your son that we'd visit my Papa so he could talk tools."

Kenneth held her close. "My boy is always throwing me off." He gave an exaggerated sigh and released her. "If you must."

Rebecca was standing when the steward rushed in. "An express, sir."

Kenneth's countenance grew grave. He read the communication and rubbed his face. "Another ship has been attacked," he said quietly.

Rebecca's eyes widened. "Not the new steam one?"

"No, but it's just a matter of time." He tapped his desk. "We may need to discuss T.H.E.T.A. business at Duke Hartwell's house party."

"Did you really think we'd make it through the two weeks without doing so?"

"No, I suppose not, but it would've been nice if he could use this event to wind down a bit."

"You might have to show him how," Rebecca said wryly. "I don't think wind down is in the duke's vocabulary."

"Never a dull moment." Kenneth chuckled. "You better leave and see to your son and his knives."

<<<>>>

Bring him
to life

When the Armstrong family moves into the beautiful garden estate of Oakes Hollow, their new neighbor declares they'll be a breath of fresh air to the neighborhood. These Armstrongs tend to buck convention, and the Fitzpatricks are ready for the customary to be modernized. A model family with title and money, the Fitzpatricks are the embodiment of establishment, and they're tiring of that mantle.

Fast forward twelve years, and an ugly form of jealousy and contention between Clive and Geoffrey Fitzpatrick emerges from the rock-like ideal. Their sibling rivalry puts sculptress, Faye Armstrong, in the middle, and the ensuing courtship ruse takes some unexpected turns.

Will the brothers carve and shape a peace? Or will everyone be shattered?

The following is an excerpt from
*Sculpting His Likeness-The Women of T.H.E.T.A.
Book 4: Faye*

PROLOGUE

Wyatt

The black iron fence before Mr. Wyatt Armstrong created a crisp contrast with the white home. It was a fashionable prospect, but seemed a disturbing metaphor for his youth, though his sister's current residence in London wasn't his childhood home. As those memories tumbled through his mind, the warm September drizzle made him damp despite the umbrella the footman held aloft.

"We're to live here, Papa?"

The high voice awoke him from his daze, and Wyatt looked down at his seven-year-old daughter, peering up at him with large, brown eyes.

"Yes, Faye, this is our new home."

His sister, Mrs. Chelsea Caldwell, and her daughter had inherited it upon her husband's death. The home had fit the gentleman, a simple, classic man with a good eye for aesthetics who'd complemented Chelsea.

"Papa, are you well?"

He mustered up a smile. *Be courageous for my brave, little lady.* "Right as a trivet. Let's go inside so you can meet your aunts and cousin."

Ordinarily, Faye would've been excited, but there'd been many upheavals in the past year, foremost her mother's death, so she was more subdued.

Faye must be exhausted. I know I am.

The butler showed them into the drawing room, outfitted in smart furnishings and well lit by a fire. Their house in Liverpool had been charming but unassuming. When his family had packed him off fifteen years ago at the age of twenty-three, they sent him away with a sizable annual allowance, but he'd settled into a simple living. Eventually he married and had wanted to scale up since he possessed the means, but his wife, Callie, insisted they were fine. His sister's home was more of the kind in which Callie's father now lived. To Faye, it was always a trip to the grand house to see her grandpapa.

"Smells like cookies," Faye remarked.

"Knowing your Aunt Chelsea, she probably has them baked all the time."

His sisters burst into the room.

"Wyatt!" shrieked Chelsea as she rushed towards him.

He hugged her fiercely. He'd never gotten along with his brothers and was a disappointment to his parents, but his sisters seemed eager to welcome him with open arms as long as he'd mended his ways. His last incident had involved the law and magistrate, which nearly ruined Chelsea's engagement.

Miss Bonnie Armstrong gave him a long hug and then stepped back and studied his daughter. "Faye?"

"Yes, my little girl."

The sisters exchanged looks, and Wyatt hugged his daughter to him.

No matter how many times he witnessed this reaction, he never got over it, though his sisters' response was mild. Faye was a well-spoken, pretty girl, and her characteristics were much like his. She had Wyatt's brown hair, only hers was curly, his brown eyes, and her complexion was not much darker than his fair one, though it held a golden undertone. The largeness of Faye's eyes came from her mother, and Wyatt loved to pinch his daughter's round, rosy cheeks. But because her mother was of African descent, her features made some people feel Faye differed from them, and that burned Wyatt up.

"Welcome, Faye," Aunt Bonnie said warmly. "We're so happy to have you here."

Chelsea beamed. "Aren't you just the cutest thing! My Daisy is a year older than you and will be so happy to have a playmate. Would you like to meet her and have some cookies?"

Faye grinned. "Indeed, I would, Aunt Chelsea."

Chelsea offered her hand and led Faye out of the room, chattering about what new dolls they'd get tomorrow.

Bonnie shook her head. "I don't know who's more excited about the dolls, Chelsea or Faye."

Wyatt laughed. *Some things never change.*

"Faye is a beautiful child and very poised for her age. You must be quite proud of her."

"Yes, she's a good girl." He grinned wryly. "Takes after her mother."

Bonnie rubbed his arm. "It's been a troublesome time, hasn't it?"

"Callie was..." Wyatt faltered, at a loss describing how bereft he was without her.

"You're here now. We'll get through together as best we can."

CHAPTER 1

A Breath of Fresh Air

Faye

DAISY CALDWELL RAN BY eleven-year-old Faye and pulled her through the enormous ornate doors of Oakes Hollow. Once inside, Daisy squealed as she ripped her bonnet off, revealing a head of fine, sandy-colored hair and brown eyes the same hue as Faye's. "I can't believe we're to live here now!" She paused. "I suppose that's wicked to say since we're here because Uncle Stewart is dead."

Faye shrugged, not knowing what to say about that. She was sorry for anyone to lose their life, but Uncle Stewart never paid her any attention, so she didn't feel his passing deeply. While Faye had been of the understanding that her aunts and Papa weren't very close to him either, his sudden death had left them somber.

"We've returned," Aunt Bonnie wryly announced as she, Papa, and Aunt Chelsea walked in behind them. Aunt Bonnie looked much like Papa, while Daisy had inherited her lighter hair and sun-kissed complexion from her mother and strongly resembled her. Papa and his two sisters had been here briefly after the funeral, so her aunt's comment struck Faye as odd, but she supposed this return was more significant.

"I can't believe I'm back here." Papa exhaled.

Aunt Chelsea chuckled. "You two make it sound like a death sentence. It wasn't so bad, and things will be completely different with Wyatt in charge and the girls here. Come on, chin up!" She flung her arms wide. "We're embarking on an epoch."

Papa gave his sister a look as Faye and Daisy giggled.

Aunt Chelsea always makes things diverting and delightful. Faye twirled in the vast foyer. She'd never been in a room so large, and it was just their entranceway.

"On the few occasions our family held events, we'd entertain guests here since the space is so large," Aunt Bonnie said. "There's a wonderful cross breeze when the front and back entrances are open on very warm summer days."

Aunt Chelsea grabbed Faye and Daisy's hands. "I'll show you the suite Bonnie and I shared."

They ran up the stairs, across the balcony, and through a door at the end of the hall.

"Here we are!" Aunt Chelsea collapsed on a bed.

Everything was decorated in white and lilac in this bedroom, which perfectly suited Aunt Chelsea.

Faye looked out the window. The sun had appeared, and the wet gardens looked like they were sparkling. They were filled with colors and all sorts of plants, trees, sculptures, archways, and paths. "This room is lovely," she whispered as she took in the expansive landscape.

She was pleased to see that Oakes Hollow had a different wonderfulness than London. Faye liked their home in London ever so much, and was hesitant to leave. For four years, they were such a merry party, and that offered some comfort after Mama had died.

When Papa had unexpectedly inherited Oakes Hollow, he warmly invited her aunts and cousin to move with them, and they accepted. Faye was glad their unique family arrangement would stay intact, for she wasn't sure what to expect of society here. New places and people made her anxious, and her father's unease increased her own.

The girls ran into the adjoining room.

"This one is larger," Daisy said. "I like it."

"Then you shall have it," Aunt Chelsea said, following them inside. "Faye, dear, would you like my old room?"

Faye nodded vigorously. Aunt Chelsea's room was much prettier.

"Faye and Chelsea will stay in this suite if you approve," Aunt Chelsea said to Papa as he walked in.

"Perfect," he replied. "That was simple."

"Papa, are we very rich, then?" Faye asked. "I feel like a princess."

Aunt Chelsea kissed her forehead.

"We have more than a few pounds, yes," he answered. "Would you and Daisy like a long walk outside? I can show you my old spots."

Faye squealed.

Aunt Bonnie ran in breathless. "Lord Yardley calls upon you, Wyatt."

Papa's eyes widened. "I didn't expect to meet him so soon. I'm sorry, girls for we'll have to postpone our walk until tomorrow."

Faye was disappointed, but this visit sounded important, and tomorrow was soon enough.

"Do I look all right? Will I embarrass you?" Papa teased his sisters.

Aunt Bonnie gave him a playful hit on the arm. "You're fine. Now go down and represent the new regime."

*****

The girls were with Aunt Chelsea in the morning room, enjoying refreshments. They weren't horribly far from London, but it had been a busy and momentous day, and the three were hungry.

Aunt Bonnie poked her head in. "Lord Yardley asked to meet the girls."

"That's quite kind of him." Aunt Chelsea put her napkin on a small end table. "Let's not keep the marquess waiting."

Faye had been in the presence of only a couple of noblemen, and she'd never been introduced to one. "Is Papa suddenly a very important man?" Faye asked her aunt as they left the room.

"To some, he might now seem so." Aunt Chelsea was unusually solemn. "But he won't change, and those who know and love him will recognize that."

Faye was pleased with that answer. She loved her Papa just as he was.

Aunt Chelsea stopped walking and studied the girls. "We Armstrongs aren't bottom of the barrel."

Daisy giggled. "I never thought the Caldwells were."

"You're an Armstrong too, and our wealth and estate rival most noblemen." Aunt Chelsea gave them a pointed look. "You two are the daughters and granddaughters of gentlemen. Don't forget that, even if others do."

Faye and Daisy exchanged looks.

Head held high, Aunt Chelsea continued walking and the girls followed. They entered the drawing room, and Faye stopped short, taking in the space with wonder. It had an attractive prospect towards the garden and was richly furnished.

"Faye!" Aunt Bonnie said urgently.

She snapped to attention.

A tall, slender man, whom Faye supposed was Lord Yardley, chuckled gently.

"Curtsy." Aunt Bonnie gave her an exasperated look.

Faye dropped into a low curtsy. She must have missed her introduction.

Daisy started giggling as Faye stared at the floor. This was a terrible beginning.

Lord Yardley crouched in front of her, his gray eyes twinkling. "It's an attractive room, isn't it, Miss Faye?"

"Yes, it is, sir," Faye replied. "I apologize for my impertinence. I'm generally much more attentive."

Lord Yardley's smile widened. "I'm delighted to have made your acquaintance. I believe we'll become good friends."

Faye grinned and curtsied again, but this time with more enthusiasm. "I'd like that."

This man doesn't look at me differently. We'll be just fine.

Lord Yardley stood and directed his attention towards Papa. "You'll have to bring the girls over. Clive was just complaining he has no one to play with."

Papa shook his hand. "I will, and thank you."

"I believe you and your family will be a breath of fresh air around here."

*****

It was a pleasantly warm day for late spring, and Faye tried to enjoy the ride to Yardley. The sky was clear with abundant sunshine and the countryside picturesque and peaceful. Nestled amongst green hills was the mansion proper, larger than Oakes Hollow.

Faye's nervousness had lessened since she'd met Lord Yardley the day before, but she didn't know what to expect of his wife and son. Daisy held her hand as they entered the massive, stately home that announced to visitors the Fitzpatricks were an established, important family.

Lady Yardley was just as kindly as her husband, and she introduced them to Clive, who was only a couple of years older than Faye. He was a nice-looking boy with brown hair, gray eyes, and a quick smile, like his father. Clive had diversions written all over his being, and Faye and Daisy began a game of hide and find with him. They played together swimmingly, and it felt like Faye had known him all her life, even though they'd just met.

She ran into a room and crouched down next to a small table. *He'll never find me here.* Something scraped the floor next to Faye and she screeched.

A tuft of golden hair poked out underneath the tablecloth.

Faye tentatively lifted the cloth and stared into the greenest eyes she'd ever seen. "Who are you?"

"Who are you?" the boy, who looked her age, asked back. "I live here."

"My name is Faye, and I'm playing hide and find with Clive."

Clive burst into the room and tackled her. "Got you! You're it."

Faye laughed and regained her balance. "Would you like to play with us?" she asked the green-eyed boy.

He glanced at the over-sized book on the floor in front of him. "I'll stay here, thank you."

Faye sat next to him under the table. "What are you looking at?"

"Pictures," he responded softly.

"Why would you want to look at boring, old books?" Clive asked.

Faye looked over the green-eyed boy's shoulder. "These are pretty."

Clive peered over the top of the book and snickered. "No wonder you're looking at it under the table. Those are the naughty art pictures Grandpapa said we shouldn't look at until we're older."

The other boy glared at him.

"I see nothing wrong with it," Faye said. "She's just

on a swing. It looks incredibly diverting"

"Maybe not that one." Clive turned the page.

"Oh," said Faye.

"That's definitely not the type of diversions we're supposed to have." Clive started making kissy faces.

Green-eyed boy slammed the book shut.

"Your turn to count, Faye. But I have to find Daisy first." Clive ran out of the room.

"I didn't mean to ruin things for you," Faye said to the other boy.

"I'm not..." He frowned. "Bad or debauched or anything."

"Of course not. I didn't think that."

"Clive made me sound like—"

Faye waved a hand. "I didn't pay him any attention. I imagine he's quite silly which should make him a fun and delightful playmate."

The boy chuckled. "He is." His grin faded. "Or used to be. I believe he's bothered by me now."

"I can't imagine anyone being bothered by you. You seem quite nice."

He gave her a shy smile. "You as well." He started leafing through the book again. "It's amazing people can dream up and make such things."

Faye pointed to a picture of a colossal sculpture. "I want to do that one day."

"I can't wait to see it."

"Are you sure you don't want to join us? You'll make four, and that's a grand number for hide and find."

He grinned. "All right then."

"I'll stay here and count."

The boy started towards the door.

"What's your name?" Faye called after him. "I assume you're Clive's brother."

He nodded. "Geoffrey. Just call me Geoff, if you please, Miss Faye."

She giggled. "You can leave off the miss. That won't do between friends."

Geoff beamed. "You're perfectly right."

*****

Geoff

Geoff ran out of the room thinking about the lovely girl with huge, brown eyes who would make magnificent, gargantuan sculptures.

Faye is going to change things.

The Women of T.H.E.T.A. series

Amid the British Industrial Revolution, players are taking their positions, and new battles are beginning — between individuals and within families, companies and industries, generations and their ideals. Relationships and loves are lost, old ones galvanized, and new ones forged.
Modern heroines
Unconventional heroes
Meet the women of T.H.E.T.A.

T.H.E.T.A. Books

Expanding Their Scope - The Women of T.H.E.T.A. Book 1: Abigail
Who Is Madalene? - The Women of T.H.E.T.A. Book 2: Hannah
The Hunt - The Women of T.H.E.T.A. Book 3: Rebecca
Sculpting His Likeness - The Women of T.H.E.T.A. Book 4: Faye
Forge - The Women of T.H.E.T.A. Book 5: Orelia

T.H.E.T.A. Novellas

The Foreman - The Women of T.H.E.T.A. Novella: Christiana (prequel)
The Imagination Room - The Women of T.H.E.T.A. Novella: Deanna (A Dr. Fiske story)

Future T.H.E.T.A. Books

The Ruins - The Women of T.H.E.T.A. Book 6: Mrs. Locke
TBD - The Women of T.H.E.T.A. Book 7: Jocelyn
TBD - The Women of T.H.E.T.A. Book 8: Portia

C.E.J., writing as Elizabeth Borae, resides in Pennsylvania, U.S.A. Besides writing, she has also worked as a literacy and mathematics tutor, specializing in working with children who have learning challenges. With a B.A. from Rutgers University majoring in Economics and Art History, she attempts to inject a little business into her stories about relationships and family during a period she loves in art and literature, the 19th century.